THE LEGEND OF DAVE THE VILLAGER 2

by Dave Villager

First Print Edition (August 2019)

BOOK TWO:
Ice and Fire

The Legend of Dave the Villager 2

PROLOGUE

Herobrine sat upon a throne of bedrock. The small castle at the top of the mountain was all built of bedrock—the only blocks in the world that couldn't be destroyed or mined. Even the most enchanted of diamond pickaxes wouldn't even make a dent on its walls. The castle had been built by the Old People, who had once ruled the three realms. They were all gone now. Long gone.

"What news do you have for me?" Herobrine asked the witch in front of him. "Have you found the villager yet?"

"No, Master," the witch said nervously. "The villager named Dave still eludes us. But we've sent word to all the witches loyal to our cause. Everyone is looking for him—he won't be able to hide much longer."

"I hope for your sake that's true," said Herobrine. "And what word from the Nether? I haven't heard from that fool Trotter in too long."

"Um, we um, think he may have been slain, Master."

The witch pulled something out of her robes: a gold staff with an emerald on the top. Herobrine recognized it immediately: it was the magic staff he had given a pigman named Trotter. Herobrine had turned the pigmen of the Nether into zombies, all except Trotter. The magic staff was to let Trotter control the zombie pigmen. Herobrine's plan had been to let Trotter rule the Nether as he wished, if he promised to lend his zombie army to Herobrine when needed.

"We think Trotter may have been slain," the witch repeated. "There were signs of a battle."

"No matter," said Herobrine, "I'm sure I'll be able to find someone else to rule the pigmen. This wretched world is full of people as greedy and ambitious as Trotter. Is there anything else?"

"No, Master," said the witch.

"Then go then," said Herobrine. "And next time, bring me better news. I want this Dave found."

"Yes, Master."

The witch climbed onto the window ledge, equipped her elytra and flew off into the sky.

Herobrine walked to the window. From up here, high up in the mountains, he could see for miles around. Biome after biome stretched out before him.

Somewhere out there was a villager named Dave who

knew the secret to finding ender portals. He was out there, and Herobrine was going to find him.

CHAPTER ONE

Nothing but Snow

Dave had been cold for the past two days, and, he
suspected, he'd be cold for many more days to come.

"Come on bros," Steve called from up ahead. "Get a
move on!"

"It's alright for him," Carl said bitterly. "He has a
horse. Why don't I have a horse?"

As annoying as Dave thought Steve was, he had to
remember that Steve had saved their lives. A huge zombie
pigman had been about to eat Dave when Steve had
arrived in the nick of time. He'd filled the giant pigman full
of arrows and saved the day.

Also to Steve's credit was that he'd stuck around to
help them. Dave had expected Steve to ride off on his
horse as soon as they were safe, but no—Steve said he'd
stay with them until they got out of the snow biome.

"The snow can be dangerous, bros," Steve had told
them. *"Especially for noobs like you."*

At first Dave had been amazed that they'd bumped into Steve at all. The last time Dave had seen Steve, Steve had been riding away on his horse, off to kill the ender dragon. Dave had been heading in the same direction—but without a horse.

Eventually Dave realized it must have been their trip through the Nether that had put them ahead of Steve. Time and space flowed differently in the Nether, Dave had read, so the small distance they'd traveled in the Nether had been the equivalent of a much bigger distance in the real world. Well, that was Dave's theory anyway.

It was starting to get dark, so Steve lit a fire and they all sat around it. There was no shelter—all they could see were endless flat plains of snow in every direction.

"How you doing, little boys?" Steve asked the three of them. "You've had a tough couple of days."

Dave was outraged.

"Steve, we're not little boys—we're grown men!"

"Oh, sorry, bro," Steve said. "No offense. I hope you've all learned your lesson though—going on adventures is only for heroes. Still, on the plus side, at least you all got to meet me—the legendary Steve!"

"Steve," Dave said, "we've met before."

"Sorry, bro," Steve said. "I meet a lot of people. It's hard to keep track of all the names."

"You blew up my village!" Dave snapped. "You blew up

my village and stole my ender eyes and you can't even remember my name!"

"Oooooh!" said Steve. "I remember you now, dude. Wallace, isn't it?"

"It's Dave!"

"Dave, of course bro. I remember now."

Dave was seething with rage. After all that had happened, how could Steve not remember him?

"I must say," said Porkins, "this is all frightfully exciting. Off on an adventure with a famous hero. Even in the Nether we've heard of you, Steve."

Steve grinned.

"Glad to hear it, Porkchops," he said. *Porkchops* was the nickname he'd given Porkins. The pigman didn't seem to mind, but Dave thought it was ridiculously rude.

"Do you even know where we're going?" Carl asked Steve. "We've been walking for two days now. When will this biome end?"

Steve laughed.

"I love this guy," he said to Porkins and Dave. "A friendly creeper! That's hilarious! You know, little dude, I almost killed you when I first saw you—I thought you were coming to blow me up!"

"Yes, I remember," Carl said bitterly. "You almost cut me in two with your sword."

Steve built them a very basic wooden house and some beds, and they all went to sleep. In the morning, Steve put the beds in his backpack, but left the rest of the blocks.

"I've got more wood than I know what to do with," Steve told them. "I'll just build a new house tomorrow night."

Dave imagined all the houses Steve must have left behind him over the years. A trail of abandoned houses in the middle of the wilderness.

They continued their journey. By midday they could see huge blue towers in the distance.

"Is that a city?" Dave asked Steve. He was imagining a city of ice skyscrapers.

"Nah, those are ice spikes," Steve said. "I dunno why they grow like that. Ice is weird."

As they got closer they could see the ice spikes more clearly: massive blue columns reaching up into the sky. Dave had to squint and put his hand up to stop the sunlight reflecting off the ice hurting his eyes.

"Good grief," said Porkins. "What a wonderful sight!"

Finally they reached the ice spikes. It was only when walking underneath them that Dave really got a sense of how huge they were. He reached out and touched the base of one of the spikes. It was cold, of course, and as hard as stone.

"Wow," he said, and he saw his breath appear in front

of his eyes as mist.

It was so cold in the ice spikes biome that Dave wished he had some warmer clothes. But at least he had clothes—Porkins and Carl were naked. Carl said the explosives inside his body kept him warm no matter the temperature outside, but Porkins was suffering. He had grown up in the Nether, so wasn't used to this sort of cold.

"I-I-I'll be o-o-ok old chap," Porkins shivered. "A little cold never hurt anyone."

But Dave could see Porkins was just putting on a brave face.

"Steve," he said, "we need to find some warmer clothing, or Porkins is going to freeze."

"A frozen pork chop!" Steve said. But no-one laughed.

"Are there any animal mobs in the snow that drop wool or leather?" Dave asked Steve.

"Rabbit hides," Steve said. "Four rabbit hides make one leather. Then we can use the leather to make your friend some armor. We just have to slay a whole bunch of rabbits."

He did some quick maths in his head.

"Hmm, two leather each for boots, then the tunic needs eight..."

"Steve," said Dave, "what are you—"

Steve held a finger up to silence him.

"Ninety-six rabbits!" Steve exclaimed. "If we slay ninety-six rabbits we should have enough leather to make your friend a full outfit."

"Good lord, that seems a bit much," said Porkins. "I'm a bit chilly, I'll admit, but ninety-six rabbits getting the chop... that's a bit harsh."

"Here comes one now," Carl said. They all turned to see what Carl was looking at. Something white and fluffy was coming towards them out of the mist.

"That's rabbit number one," Carl grinned. "Get your sword out, Porkins. Only ninety-five left after this."

"That's a big rabbit," Porkins said.

"I don't think it's a rabbit," Dave said. He drew his sword.

Finally the creature emerged from the mist—Dave was about to charge it with his sword, but then stopped. It was a polar bear—but only a baby one.

"Aw, what a cute little chap!" Porkins said. He ran forward and rubbed the top of the bear's head. "You're a good chap, aren't you. A very good chap."

"It would make a nice coat," Carl said.

"Carl!" Porkins said, outraged.

"Maybe we should get out of here," Dave said. "What if its mum and dad are nearby?"

"Don't worry my man," Steve said. "There's four of us

here. If anything comes at us we can face it together!"

ROOOOAAARRRR!!!!!

They all looked round and saw a huge white bear charging towards them through the mist. This one was no baby.

"Every man for himself!" Carl yelled, as he ran off in the opposite direction.

CHAPTER TWO

Bear!

Dave froze like a cow in torchlight. The bear was almost upon him, but he hadn't even drawn his sword.

But Steve had no such problem. He whipped his sword out and charged at the bear head on.

"No!" Dave heard Porkins yell.

Porkins dived forward and tackled Steve to the ground.

"What are you doing, bro?!" Steve yelled.

"You can't kill it!" yelled Porkins. "Not in front of its cub!"

Dave had forgotten about the little bear, but before he had time to think about it he heard Porkins scream. The mother bear was in front of Porkins and Steve, standing up on its back legs and getting ready to attack.

Dave pulled out his diamond sword. He didn't want to slay the bear, but it looked like he had little choice—if the bear wasn't stopped it would eat Steve and Porkins—and almost certainly have him and Carl for dessert.

"Over here, you... bear!" he yelled.

The polar bear, still standing up, turned to look at Dave, its teeth bared. Then it got back on all fours and charged right for him.

ROOOOAAARRR!!!

Dave froze again. He tried to get his sword ready, but his hand was trembling.

This was a terrible idea, he thought to himself. *This was a terrible, terrible idea!*

The bear was almost on him now. Dave brought his sword up to block its attack, but suddenly he felt his hand go numb from nerves, and the sword fell from his fingers. He watched in horror as it plunged into the snow.

It was too late to pick the sword back up. Dave just closed his eyes and braced himself for the bear's attack.

"It's Steve time!"

Dave opened his eyes and saw Steve run in front of him, blocking the bear's path. But Steve, idiot that he was, didn't even have his sword drawn!

Then, moving more quickly than Dave would have thought possible, Steve started to build. He built a wall of wooden blocks to shield Dave and himself from the bear. Dave could hear the bear scratching and pounding on the other side, roaring with frustration.

The bear wasn't stupid though, and Dave soon heard it

making its way round the side of the wall—but Steve was too quick for it. He built a wall round the side, then another, then another, completely trapping the mother bear and her cub inside.

"There you go," Steve said proudly to Porkins, "I didn't kill it."

Porkins got back to his feet. Carl, who had run as far away as his tiny creeper legs could carry him, made his way back towards them.

"That was awesome," Carl grinned. Dave was shocked —Carl never normally had a kind word to say about anyone.

"But we can't just leave them in there," Porkins said.

"How come?" Steve asked.

"Because they've got no food, old chap!" said Porkins. "And they need room to run around and be free."

Steve thought for a moment.

"I have an idea!" he said. He started building— replacing two of the wall blocks with a steel door (quickly so that the polar bears couldn't get out) then getting some red powder out of his bag and adding it to some contraptions Dave didn't recognize.

"What's all that stuff?" Carl asked.

"Redstone," said Steve. "I'll create a circuit, leave a trail of redstone, then we can flip a switch and open the door from a safe distance."

Dave had read a little about redstone in his crafting book, but he'd never tried building anything. Steve was using the redstone like he'd done this a million times before. It looked really complicated to Dave, but Steve seemed to have no problem.

"Come on, bros," Steve said, "we need to get a safe distance away."

They followed behind as he led them away from the polar bear enclosure, leaving a trail of redstone across the snow. He led them to a small ledge in the shadow of an ice spike, then he put down a lever. A unbroken trail of red powder led all the way across the snow to the metal door.

"Would you like to do the honors, Pork Chop?" Steve asked Porkins.

"How fun!" said Porkins, taking hold of the lever. "Tally ho!"

Porkins pulled the lever. There was a couple of seconds delay, then the metal door opened. Dave and the others watched as the polar bear and her cub cautiously stuck their noses out of the door, then, seeing that the coast was clear, they began to walk off across the snow.

"Nice one, Steve," Carl whispered.

"Yes, well done old chap!" Porkins added.

"Yeah, well done Steve," said Dave. He tried to smile, but he found it difficult. Dave didn't feel happy for the polar bears or happy they'd all survived. He just felt jealous. Jealous of Steve.

CHAPTER THREE

Finding Shelter

Dave hated feeling this way, but he couldn't help it. Steve was effortlessly heroic, whether fighting off giant zombie pigmen or trapping polar bears, and that made Dave jealous. He had thought that he'd return from his adventure as a great hero, but once again he'd been overshadowed by Steve.

It didn't help that Porkins and Carl spent the rest of the day talking with Steve, listening to his stories as they walked through the snow.

"This one time I fought a skeleton riding a spider!" Steve told them. "I blocked its arrows with my shield—*thuck thuck thuck!*—then ran over and chopped its head off. Both of them!"

"Yeah right," said Dave bitterly. "Skeletons don't ride spiders."

"This one did, little dude," Steve insisted. And he went on telling his story.

Even Carl, who normally just made sarcastic comments and complained, was fawning over Steve—asking him about the mobs he'd slain and the treasure he'd found.

By the time night began to set in, Dave was thoroughly miserable.

"Ok bros," Steve said, "looks like I ought to build us a house for the night."

"Sounds good, old bean," said Porkins, smiling. The pigman was a lot happier now: after the polar bear incident, Steve had rummaged around in his bag and found he did have some leather after all. There was enough of it to make Porkins a tunic, some pants and some boots, so he was much warmer now.

Steve was getting ready to lay the wooden blocks down for the house when Dave spotted something in the distance.

"What's that over there?" he asked the others. "It looks like some sort of building."

Hidden in the mist was a small domed structure. Dave and the others walked forward until finally they could see what it was: a little building made of blocks of snow.

"Hey it's an igloo," Steve said. "I love these little things!"

Dave rolled his eyes. Of course Steve had seen one before—Steve had seen *everything* before.

But he hasn't been to the End, Dave thought to himself. *And he hasn't slain an ender dragon. I can be the one to do those things first!*

Steve led them into the igloo.

"It's a little cozy, but it'll do for a night," Steve said.

There was only one bed in the igloo, but Steve got three more out from his backpack. It was a bit cozy, but at least they all had somewhere to sleep.

As they all lay in bed, trying to get to sleep, Dave had a sudden thought.

"Steve," he said, "how many of my eyes of ender do you have left?"

"Eyes of what-now?" asked Steve.

"Eyes of ender," Dave repeated, trying not to lose his temper. "Ender eyes. Those green eye stone things you stole from me back at the stronghold."

"I'm still drawing a blank, dude."

"They show the way to ender portals!" Dave snapped. "I had some but you stole them all off me and rode away on your horse!"

"Oh those," said Steve. "I sold them for Emeralds. Well, an emerald. A villager in a desert biome gave me one emerald for the whole lot. Pretty sweet deal, huh?"

Dave was furious.

"Do you know how hard they are to make? How

difficult the ingredients are to get? I would have given you an emerald to keep them! I would have given you a hundred emeralds!"

"Little bro," Steve said, "you need to learn to bargain."

"So how are you planning on finding another portal?" Dave snapped.

"Yeah, I was wondering that," said Steve. "The past couple of weeks I've just been riding around, hoping to come across some more of those end eye things, but no luck. Could you tell me how to craft them?"

Dave couldn't help but smile. So Steve, who knew so much, didn't know the recipe for eyes of ender. That meant he'd never find another stronghold—Dave would be the first to find another end portal and slay the ender dragon!

"Sorry," Dave told him, "I've forgotten the recipe."

Dave pulled the covers around him tighter, getting nice and snug. He couldn't help but smile: finally he had an advantage over Steve!

And then he heard the banging.

"Can anyone else hear that?" he asked the others.

"All I can hear is you not letting me get to sleep," said Carl.

"I can't hear anything, bro," said Steve.

"That's because you're talking!" snapped Dave. "Just listen!"

Remarkably, the other three shut up for once and did listen.

It was unmistakable now: a very faint noise:

Bang bang bang bang...

"I... I think it's coming from under the floor," said Carl, sounding terrified.

CHAPTER FOUR

Under the Igloo

They all peered over the sides of their beds, looking at the floor.

"Maybe there's a cave under the igloo," Porkins whispered. "A cave full of ruddy zombies!"

The noise was coming from under the plush white rug. Still lying on his bed, Dave reached over and pulled the rug slowly up...

"There's something here," Dave said. He pulled the rug to the side, revealing a wooden trapdoor.

"A secret base!" whispered Porkins. "What fun!"

"Cool!" said Steve. "Let's have a look!"

"Wait!" said Dave. "It could be dangerous!"

But Steve wasn't one for waiting. Before Dave knew it, Steve was through the trapdoor, climbing down a previously-unseen ladder.

Dave, Porkins and Carl jumped out of their beds and dashed over to the trapdoor, watching as Steve made his way down the ladder.

"What fun!" said Porkins, and he started climbing down too.

"After you," Carl said to Dave.

Dave rolled his eyes, but then started climbing down the ladder as well.

"Help!" he heard a voice say from below. It didn't sound like either Porkins or Steve. "Please help me!"

"It's ok bro," Dave heard Steve saying. "The heroes have arrived!"

Dave reached the bottom of the ladder. He was in a small stone room, a chest on one side, a table covered in strange equipment on the other, but that wasn't what caught his attention.

At the far end of the room were two tiny prison cells, sealed off from the rest of the room by metal bars. Inside one cell was a villager. Inside the other cell was a zombie. But not just any zombie—it looked like a cross between a zombie and a villager. A *zombie villager*.

Dave was shocked. He'd heard that villagers could get infected by zombies, but he'd never seen a zombie villager with his own eyes. It looked just like a normal villager, but with green skin and ragged clothes.

"BUUUUURRR!" said the zombie villager.

"Please," said the normal villager. "You have to let me out!"

25

Steve took out a diamond pickaxe and started hacking away at the bars. Before long the villager was free.

"Thank you!" the villager said. "Thank you, Thank you!" Then: "Hey, I know you—you're Steve, right?"

Steve grinned. "The one and only."

"Wow," said the villager. "It's so awesome to meet you. You're almost as big a hero as Ripley."

And with that, the villager dashed up the ladder, yelling "I'm free, I'm free!"

Steve looked confused. Maybe even a little hurt.

"Who's Ripley?" he wondered.

"BUUUUUUR!" said the zombie villager.

Dave took another look round the room. For the first time he noticed a sign above the two prison cells—two arrows, each facing in opposite directions.

"What do those arrows mean?" he wondered.

Steve took a look at the sign. "I guess it's showing that villagers can turn into zombies."

"That explains the arrow going from the zombie to the villager," Dave said, "but not the arrow going the other way."

"Whatever," said Steve. "Let's see if there's any loot!"

He opened the chest and started rummaging through.

"There's a lot of junk in here," he said, throwing items over his shoulder. "Ah nice, a golden apple!"

He held up the most beautiful apple that Dave had ever seen. Instead of having red skin, the apple had skin that looked like solid gold. Dave could see his own face reflecting back at him.

"I wonder what it tastes like?" Steve said. He opened his mouth, ready to take a bite.

"WAIT!" Dave shouted.

"What's the matter, old chap?" Porkins asked.

Dave went over to the table. On it were a few scraps of paper with scruffy writing and diagrams on them.

"Well, can I eat it or not, bro?" Steve asked.

Dave looked through the papers.

"I think we may be able to turn the zombie back into a villager," Dave said. "It's hard to read this writing, but I think these are instructions. Steve, what ingredients were in that chest? I think we've got to do some brewing."

With Steve's help, Dave brewed a potion. It was his first time using a brewing stand, but, naturally, Steve knew exactly what to do.

"Ok," Dave said, looking at the bottle in his hand, "this is a Splash Potion of Weakness. We have to throw it over the zombie to weaken him, then feed him the golden apple. If these notes are correct, he should turn back to normal."

"Who was doing all these zombie experiments anyway?" Porkins wondered. "You don't think it was

Herobrine again?"

"I guess if this works we can ask this guy," Dave said, nodding his head towards the zombie villager. "It's a shame his friend ran off so quickly."

"Do you... do you think this would work on zombie pigmen too?" Porkins asked, his voice cracking slightly. Dave knew that Porkins wanted more than anything to turn his people—the pigmen—back to normal.

"Maybe," Dave said. He had no idea if it would or not, and he didn't want to get Porkins's hopes up too much.

"There's only one problem," Steve said. He took the apple and tried to push it through the bars. "The apple's too big to fit through."

"Then we'll have to break the bars," Dave said. "Porkins, you throw the potion over the zombie, then Steve, you break the bars with your pickaxe. Then I'll... I'll give the zombie the golden apple."

"You're just going to hand it to him?" Porkins asked nervously. "You really think that'll work, old chap?"

Dave wasn't sure at all. But they had to try. If an innocent villager had been turned into a zombie they had to save him. Or her. It was hard to tell if the zombie was a boy or a girl.

"Ok," said Dave, "everyone ready?"

Everyone was.

"Porkins, throw the potion!"

Porkins thrust his hand forward, splashing the potion through the bars, all over the zombie.

"BUUUUUURRR!!!"

The zombie flailed around for a bit, but then it calmed down again. It looked sleepy, like it could barely keep its eyes open.

"Steve, break the bars!" yelled Dave.

Steve smashed through the bars with his diamond pickaxe. Dave braced himself, ready for the zombie villager to rush out, but it just stayed in its cell, staring at the floor.

"Buuuuur..." the zombie muttered sleepily.

Dave gingerly stepped forward, holding the golden apple out in front of him.

"H-here you go," he said to the zombie. "Would you like a snack?"

The zombie villager lifted its head and looked curiously at the apple.

"Come on," Dave said. "Take it. It's for you."

The zombie slowly lifted its hand.

"That's right," said Dave. "A lovely golden apple!"

Finally the zombie took the apple.

"Buuur?" It said.

"Now eat it," Dave said. "It's lovely!"

The zombie took a bite, it's teeth crunching through

the apple's golden skin. From the outside the Apple had looked like solid gold, but it looked like it was as soft and easy to eat as a normal apple.

The zombie villager's face lit up, and it took another bite. Then another, then another, until the apple was all gone."

"Nothing's happening, bro," Steve whispered.

"Buuur?" The zombie said.

Then, suddenly, its body started twisting and contorting, flailing around and smashing into the walls of the cell.

"What's it doing?" Porkins asked. "Is it trying to dance?"

"No," said Dave, "I think it's transforming."

He was right. The zombie's green skin was fading to pink, and the noises it was making sounded less zombie now and more villager.

"BUUUURRR!!" It groaned. "BUUUURRR! BUUUURRR! BUUUU—ooow, what's happening to me?!"

Finally it collapsed on the ground, breathing heavily.

"Did it work?" Porkins asked.

The villager raised its head—a zombie no more.

"Where am I?" the villager asked. It was a woman, probably just a couple of years younger than Dave's mother. Dave felt a sudden pang in his chest—he hoped that wherever his mom and dad were they were doing ok.

"You were, um, turned into a zombie," Dave told her. "Do you know who did this to you?"

"No idea," the woman said. "The last thing I remember was going for a walk in the snow with my husband and then I was here, in front of you."

"I say, so you don't remember being a zombie at all?" Porkins asked.

"Nope," said the woman.

"There was another villager in the cell next to yours," Dave said, "but he ran off as soon as we freed him, so we couldn't ask him if he knew who did this."

The woman's face darkened.

"The other villager... was he wearing blue robes?"

"Er yes," said Dave.

"That rat!" the woman snarled. "That's my good-for-nothing husband! Are you telling me he just ran off and left me?!"

"Afraid so," said Dave.

"I'll kill him!" said the woman. "I'll make him wish he was never spawned!"

"Wait," said Porkins suddenly, "can you hear something? Up in the igloo?"

They all listened.

"It's Carl," said Dave. "It sounds like he's talking to

someone."

They all climbed the ladder. Carl and the villager—the one who'd run away when they freed him—were sitting on one of the beds eating baked potatoes and chatting away.

"Hello!" said the villager happily when he saw Dave, Porkins and Steve come up the ladder. "I was just talking to your little friend here. He's ever so funny!"

Suddenly the villager's face dropped as he saw the woman villager come up the ladder behind the others.

"Oh," said the villager, looking terrified, "hello dear, so good to see you."

"You ran off and left your own wife as a zombie!" the woman villager yelled. "What kind of husband are you!"

"I didn't know it was you dear, I swear!" said the man villager, backing away across the room.

Carl rolled his eyes.

"Why can't we ever meet some nice, normal people?" he asked Dave.

CHAPTER FIVE
Phillip and Liz

So the six of them continued the journey through the snow. The man villager, unfortunately, knew nothing about who'd captured them: just like his wife, the last thing he remembered before waking up in the cell was walking through the snow. As far as he could tell, he and his wife had been down in the igloo's secret basement for around two days when Dave and his friends found them, and no-one else had been down to the cellar in all that time.

"Unless they came down when I was sleeping," the villager said. "I am a deep sleeper."

The man villager was called Phillip and the woman villager was Liz. They lived in a town nearby, and they told Dave and the others they'd get a warm welcome there.

"Of course I recognized you straight away," Liz said to Steve. "The legendary Steve! There's a huge statue in our town of you, made of solid gold! We put it up after you saved us from that creeper attack, all those years ago."

"Of course," said Steve, "how could I forget!"

Although it sounded to Dave like Steve didn't remember at all.

"Although it's not as big as the new statue," Phillip told them, "the one of Ripley."

Liz rolled her eyes.

"My husband is always on about Ripley. Ripley this, Ripley that—it's all he ever speaks about!"

"What is Ripley?" Dave asked.

"You mean you've never heard of Ripley?" said Phillip, sounding amazed.

"Nope," said Dave.

"Why, he's our town's hero!" Phillip said. "He's an even bigger hero than Steve! Uh, no offense."

But Steve did look offended. It made Dave smile, seeing Steve uncomfortable like this. Everywhere Steve went people told him what a great hero he was, and now this villager was saying there was an even *bigger* hero.

"I'd sure like to meet this Ripley," said Steve bitterly. "Then we'll see who the best hero is."

"Ripley is amazing!" Phillip went on, oblivious to Steve's annoyance. "He defeated a horde of skeletons the other week. Then he fought off a spider attack. Then he obliterated a zombie invasion. A lot of bad guys have been trying to have a pop at our village recently, but Ripley beats them every time!"

"Is Ripley a villager?" Dave asked.

"Yep," said Phillip happily. "The greatest villager who ever lived!"

Dave couldn't believe it. *A villager hero!* He had to meet this Ripley.

By late afternoon they could see Phillip and Liz's town in the distance. It was built at the foot of a huge mountain. It looked much bigger than Dave's old village, with tall wooden houses and cobbled streets lit by lamps.

By the time they made it to the town it was night. The town was bathed in a sheen of pale blue moonlight. It was one of the most beautiful sights Dave had ever seen.

"Welcome to Snow Town," Phillip grinned.

"It's absolutely spiffing!" said Porkins, looking on in amazement.

They had almost reached the edge of the town when two villagers on horseback rode out to meet them.

"Who goes there?" one of the riders asked.

"Barry, it's me!" said Phillip.

"Phillip!" said the rider. "We've been looking for you and Liz for days. Where've you been—it's been a week!"

"Has it really been that long?" said Phillip. "Well, it was quite an adventure, I can tell you."

"Yes, yes," said Liz. "It was all such marvelous fun. I got turned into a zombie and abandoned by my husband. What an adventure!"

"I didn't abandon you!" insisted Phillip.

"And who are you?" the rider said, turning to Dave and his friends before he could get caught up in Phillip and Liz's argument. "A creeper!" he yelled, catching sight of Carl. He drew an iron sword. "Stay back!"

"No," said Dave, "he's our friend—I promise."

The guard didn't look convinced.

"I friendly creeper? I've never heard of such a thing."

"Well, you have now," said Carl. "Do you mind putting that sword away?"

The guard reluctantly sheathed his sword.

"My apologies," he said. "These are dark times. Our town has been besieged by monsters of late. If it wasn't for Ripley—"

"Bro," said Steve angrily, stepping forward, "I don't want to hear another word about this Ripley!"

"Steve!" the rider exclaimed. "I'm sorry sir, I didn't see you there. What an honor!"

Steve grinned.

"Always nice to meet a fan."

"Come on Barry," said the second rider, "let's take them in. It looks like a storm's on its way."

He was right, Dave saw. It had started to snow again.

The two riders led Dave and the others into the town. Dave, Porkins and Carl looked round in amazement at the beautiful wooden buildings: huge lodges with sloped roofs and balconies. When they reached a fork in the cobbled street, Phillip and Liz turned to speak to them.

"Well, our house is down here," Phillip said. "I suspect you'll want to stay at the inn, so we'll say our goodbyes for now."

"Thanks again for saving me," Liz said. "You four really are heroes."

"Although not as much as Ripley," Phillip added.

Liz rolled her eyes. The two of them made their way down a cobbled street.

"If I hear you say one more word about Ripley—" Liz said, and then she and Phillip disappeared around a corner.

"Come on," one of the riders said to Dave and the others. "The inn is this way."

They followed the riders down a narrow street, then suddenly they came out into a huge town square, surrounded by important-looking stone buildings. But it wasn't the fancy buildings that caught Dave's eye: it was the statues.

In the middle of the square was a huge gold-block statue of a man holding a sword: it was clearly meant to be

Steve. But next to it, almost twice the size, was a statue made of diamond blocks—this one was of a villager, also holding a sword. The size of the villager statue made the smaller Steve statue look like it was of a little kid.

"Dude!" said Steve, sounding outraged. "How come that statue's bigger than mine?"

"That's Ripley," said one of the riders, "our town's hero."

The riders led them to a large inn on the other side of town. It took a lot of convincing by Dave for the inn-keep to let Carl in ("he'll blow my inn to pieces!" she insisted), but eventually they managed to hire a couple of rooms. Dave, Porkins and Carl didn't have many emeralds, so they all had to share a room. The inn-keep gave Steve the best room she had for free—as he'd apparently saved her from zombies when she was a little girl.

"What an adventure this is!" Porkins said, when he, Dave and Carl were finally alone in their room. Dave and Porkins both had beds and Carl, as he was so small, was sleeping in an open drawer.

"I guess," said Dave. His passion for adventure had worn a bit thin over the past few days. He'd liked it when it was just him, Porkins and Carl together, but Steve was ruining things. He was so good at everything that Dave and the others might as well have been spectators.

"Dave, old bean," said Porkins, "do you think that

golden apple technique would work on my people? Maybe that's how I can finally turn them all back into normal pigmen."

"Maybe," said Dave. "I tell you what—let's collect as much gold and apples as we can, and when we've got enough, we'll return to the Nether and try it out."

"A spiffing idea!" said Porkins happily. "Very spiffing indeed!"

Soon the pigman and Carl were both fast asleep, leaving Dave to his thoughts.

We need to find some endermen, Dave thought to himself. *If we're going to build more eyes of ender, we need ender pearls.*

With all the distractions of recent days, Dave hadn't thought about his quest to slay the Ender Dragon in a while, but he hadn't given up. Their trip to the Nether had provided them with plenty of blaze powder—even if they'd nearly died getting it—so now all they needed were ender pearls, then they could build eyes of ender and find their way to another fortress.

It all sounds so simple, Dave thought—Although he knew by now that nothing about his adventure was ever simple.

CHAPTER SIX

The Wither

Dave was woken by the sound of explosions. He sat up in bed and saw Porkins and Carl were awake too. Porkins was looking out of the window.

"What's going on?" Dave asked.

"The town is burning!" said Porkins.

Dave jumped out of bed and ran over to the window. He could see the endless wooden rooftops of Snow Town stretching into the distance, and in the middle of them a fire was burning. Every few seconds an explosion would go off, sending blocks of wood flying into the air.

"We have to help," Dave said. "Come on!"

"Do we really?" asked Carl. "This bed is so comfy." But once Dave gave him a stern look he got out of bed and joined them.

Dave opened the door of their room and the first thing he saw was Steve, dressed head to toe in his diamond armor.

"Don't worry little bros," he said. "I'm on my way. Steve to the rescue!"

"Stop showing off and just get moving!" Dave yelled.

So the four of them ran out of the inn and down the cobblestone streets towards the fires. Carl only had little legs, so he rode on Porkins's shoulders.

"I can't believe we're running *towards* the danger," said Carl. "Everyone knows you run *away* from danger— that's the normal thing to do!"

"A creeper afraid of explosions?" said Dave, grinning. "Who would have thought?"

"Hey, we like to explode on our own terms," said Carl. "Creeper culture is very complex—I wouldn't expect a villager to understand."

They finally reached the fire. A group of buildings had been destroyed; their blocky ruins still burning. In the middle of the destruction were a group of villagers, holding bows and iron swords and looking very nervous.

"Why have they got swords?" Dave wondered. "Are they planning on chopping the fire's head off?"

But then his question was answered, as a huge monster floated out of the ruins of a burning building.

Dave had seen pictures of this type of monster before, but seeing one in the flesh was quite different. Its body was like a long, black spine, oily and slimy looking. It had no arms and legs, but floated through the air without wings.

And on the top of its shoulders were three oily black skulls.

A whither.

The wither's middle skull—the largest—opened its jaws wide, making a horrible screaming sound, and a ball of fire spat from its jaws. The fireball hit the ground near the villagers, causing a huge explosion but—thankfully— missing them.

Suddenly the wither turned, facing Dave and his friends. It opened its mouth and spat out another fireball— although Dave realized that they weren't fireballs after all, but skulls!

"Take cover!" Dave shouted. He, Porkins, Carl and Steve all dived out of the way as the skull hit the ground and exploded.

"Steve, do something!" said Carl. "Have you fought one of these things before?"

"No," said Steve, "but how hard can it be? I'm Steve!"

Steve ran forward in his diamond armor, clutching his diamond sword. Dave had to admire Steve's bravery, even if his common sense left a lot to be desired.

"Have at thee!" Steve yelled. He swung his sword at the wither, but it rose into the air, dodging his swing.

"Think you can escape me up there?" Steve yelled. He took off his backpack and rummaged around, looking for something. "Uh oh," he said, "I don't suppose anyone has a spare bow? I think I left mine back at the inn."

"Porkins, do you have your bow?" Dave asked.

"Sorry old bean," said Porkins, "I left it back at the room!"

The wither screamed again, spitting out skulls in all directions. Dave dodged an explosion just in time, hiding behind the broken wall of a ruined building.

Then he heard the hooves.

"It's Ripley!" Dave heard someone yell. "We're saved!"

Dave peered over the wall and saw a horseman riding towards the wither. Both horse and rider were clad in diamond armor. The horse reared up and the rider aimed his bow at the wither. The rider's armor and bow were all pulsating with purple light—enchantments.

The rider fired an arrow at the wither. The wither screamed in frustration and fired a barrage of flaming skulls back, but the rider was too quick, pulling at the reigns of his horse and dodging out of the way just in time.

Next the rider jumped off of his horse to the ground, and fired more arrows at the wither, his fingers working the bow so fast that Dave could barely keep track. Arrow after arrow hit the wither, each one making it scream with pain and fury.

The wither, perhaps realizing that ranged attacks weren't working, flew down towards the rider, but the rider was ready—he drew his sword and sliced the wither's heads off: one, two, three. The wither flailed around headless for a few seconds, then it—and its three severed heads—all went *poof* and were gone. All that was left was a shining star-like object. The rider picked it up and pocketed it, then took off his helmet.

It was a villager.

CHAPTER SEVEN

Ripley

"Ripley, you saved us!" one of the villagers yelled happily. Soon the diamond-armored villager—Ripley—was surrounded by a crowd of grateful people.

"Thank you Ripley!" another villager said. "You're the best!"

Ripley smiled. It wasn't an arrogant smile, like the one Steve always wore, but a nice one. A *kind* smile.

"Is everyone alright?" Ripley asked. "Did everyone get out ok?"

It turned out that everyone had. The wither had appeared suddenly in the center of the village, no-one knew where from.

"It could have teleported in from the Nether," one villager suggested.

"Withers don't come from the Nether," said Porkins. "Only wither skeletons."

"Where *do* withers come from?" Dave wondered, but

nobody knew—not even Steve.

A jolly, fat villager in crimson robes soon waddled over, bowing down before Ripley.

"You've saved us again!" the fat villager said. "We'll build another statue of you, Ripley—twice the size of the old one!"

Ripley laughed. "There's no need, Mr Mayor, honestly."

The mayor suddenly noticed Steve.

"Well I never!" he said. "Is that... Steve?!"

"The one and only, bro," said Steve, stepping forward. "You know, I would have taken care of that monster myself, but sometimes I like to let others have their chance too. It's only fair."

"Two great heroes in our little town!" The mayor said excitedly. "What an honor! We'll have a banquet tonight to celebrate—everyone is invited!"

Everyone cheered.

"Oh," said the mayor, "and, er, someone fix those broken homes please."

That night the mayor was as good as his word—putting on a banquet in the square for the whole town. Long tables had been set out around the two statues, and there was a table of honor at the front, which Dave and his friends somehow found themselves on.

"You must try this, it's delicious," the mayor told

Dave, passing him a bowl of meat. "Only the best food for our honored guests."

Dave was about to take a piece of meat when he caught sight of Porkins, sitting next to him.

"Oh yummy!" said Porkins, taking the bowl. "This looks lovely!"

"Uh, I wouldn't if I were you," said Dave. "It's pork."

"Oh," said Porkins, looking sheepishly at the meat, his face turning a little pale. He quickly passed the bowl on.

Carl had been seated next to Ripley, near the center of the table. Apparently, Dave had overheard someone say, the mayor loved the novelty of a talking creeper so much that he wanted him close enough to talk to.

Carl was on good form, chatting away happily with Ripley and the mayor. One person who didn't look happy, however, was Steve. He'd been placed right at the end of the table, next to a fat boy who looked like he must be the mayor's son—or, at the very least, a nephew.

Then Dave felt a hand on his shoulder. He turned around and, to his surprise, saw Ripley standing behind him.

"Dave, isn't it? Can I have a word?"

Dave nodded, feeling unnaturally nervous.

Ripley led Dave away from the feast, down some narrow streets until they reached a tiny park, with a balcony that overlooked the endless icy plains below. In the distance Dave could just make out the ice spikes he and the others had walked through a few days ago.

"This is a beautiful view," said Dave.

"It is," agreed Ripley. "Dave, I was talking with your friend Carl earlier. He told me about the quest you're on— to kill a dragon."

"Oh," said Dave, feeling slightly embarrassed. He suddenly expected Ripley to tell him how stupid the idea was; that Dave should stick to being a normal villager.

"I think it's a brilliant idea," Ripley said. "So many villagers are content to lead boring, meaningless lives. We need more villagers like you, Dave. Heroes and adventurers."

"Uh thanks," said Dave, surprised. "But I'm no hero. I can barely use a sword."

"There's more to being a hero than fighting," Ripley said. "Your friend Steve needs to remember that."

"Steve's not my friend," Dave told Ripley. "He blew up my village with TNT. No reason—he just thought it would be fun to watch it explode. It was a miracle no-one was hurt."

"That sounds like Steve, alright," Ripley said. "If he's not your friend, how did you end up traveling with him?"

Dave told Ripley about his adventure so far: about Steve stealing his eyes of ender, meeting Porkins and Carl then going to the Nether, before Steve defeated the giant zombie pigman in the snow.

"As much as I dislike Steve, he has saved my life. More than once," Dave said.

Ripley nodded.

"No-one would doubt Steve's fighting prowess, but keep an eye on him," he told Dave. "Steve doesn't care about friends or about treating people with respect. I know he seems harmless, but he sees villagers as animals, not as equals."

Dave thought Ripley was probably right.

"So how did you get into the hero business?" Dave asked Ripley. "And how did you get so good at fighting?"

"It wasn't easy, I can tell you," Ripley grinned. "Villagers aren't natural fighters, as you probably know yourself. It all started about a year ago, when our town was attacked by zombies. Most people wanted to flee, saying there was no way we could defeat them without Steve, but I decided to take a stand. I crafted myself a sword, a bow and some arrows and took the fight to the zombies. It was a close thing, but somehow I defeated them. Ever since then I've been training and honing my skills. Here, let me show you something."

Ripley led Dave back down the path, this time going a different route and ending up outside a small wooden house.

"This is my home," said Ripley. "It's not much to look at, but wait til you see what I've got in the basement."

They went round to the side of the house, where a trapdoor had been built into the floor. Ripley opened the trapdoor and descended down a ladder. Dave followed. He felt a bit of a fool, following a stranger into their mysterious basement, but there was something trustworthy about Ripley.

Down, down, they went. It was almost pitch dark now, but Dave kept going..

"Nearly there," he heard Ripley say below him.

Suddenly Dave felt his feet touch solid ground.

"Ripley?" he called. It was so dark that he couldn't see a thing.

"Check this out," he heard Ripley say.

There was the *clunk* of a button being pressed and suddenly there was light.

"Wow," said Dave.

CHAPTER EIGHT

The Underground Room

They were inside a huge underground room—much larger than the house above. The walls were lined with iron blocks, and all around the room were levers and contraptions and structures.

In the middle of the room was a wide open space, an arena, with a selection of weapons leaning against a stand.

"What is all this?" Dave asked.

"This is my training room," said Ripley, smiling. "Let me show you."

Ripley went over to the weapons rack and picked up a weapon Dave hadn't seen before: it looked like a giant fork made of diamond. Next Ripley pressed a button, and suddenly four devices around the side of the arena were spitting out eggs of different colors. When the eggs hit the ground they turned into mobs.

Suddenly Ripley was surrounded by creepers and zombies, but he seemed completely unfazed.

He threw the diamond-fork-thing through the air and its three prongs lodged into a zombie's forehead. The zombie disappeared with a *Burrr!* and the fork-thing whizzed through the air, back into Ripley's hand. He threw the fork again, this time at a creeper, then grabbed a sword. Another creeper slid up to him and started hissing, but Ripley was too quick—slicing it to pieces with his sword before it could explode.

Ripley moved faster than Dave would have thought possible, hacking and slashing as more and more mobs tried to attack him. Finally all the mobs were dead, and Ripley stood victorious in the middle of piles of gunpowder and zombie flesh.

"Wow," said Dave, "that was incredible."

"That's only easy mode," Ripley grinned. He pressed another button and suddenly the blocks at the center of the arena slid away, revealing a pool of lava below. "A bit of lava always makes training sessions interesting," he grinned. "This whole town is built above a lava lake."

"Did you build all this yourself?" Dave asked.

Ripley nodded. "All my own designs. A year ago I'd never even heard of redstone, but I read every book about it I could find. It's amazing what you can build. I knew that if I was going to be a hero I couldn't be content with just learning to fight—I had to learn to craft as well. Potion brewing, enchanting, knowing how to craft armor and weapons—I taught myself everything."

Dave was impressed.

"This is what I'm most proud of though," Ripley said. He pressed a button and a panel slid open, revealing a villager who looked just like Ripley. "Meet Robo-Ripley," he said.

"Wait," said Dave, "you're telling me that's a robot? It looks so real!"

"Yep," said Ripley proudly, "it's a robot powered by redstone. He makes an excellent sparring partner. Watch."

Ripley took a sword from the rack and threw it to Robo-Ripley, who caught it without even looking.

"Engage battle mode," said Ripley.

Robo-Ripley raised its sword and put its legs shoulder width apart, taking a fighting stance.

"*Battle mode initiated*," said Robo-Ripley. "*Kill mode off.*"

"Kill mode?" asked Dave nervously.

"I thought it might make things interesting if it was actually trying to kill me," said Ripley. He grinned. "But so far I've never been brave enough to leave kill mode on."

Ripley ran forward and sliced at the robot with his sword. Robo-Ripley dodged and partied Ripley's blow with its own sword. The two of them fought an epic battle, sword clashing against sword, until finally Ripley hit the robot's sword so hard that it flew out of its hand.

Ripley raised his sword, holding the sharp point up to the robot's neck.

"I win," said Ripley.

"*Surrender mode activated,*" said the robot.

"So what now?" Dave asked. "Are you going to stay in Snow Town?"

"Not forever," Ripley said, putting his sword back on the rack. He pressed a button on Robo-Ripley's back and it returned to its cupboard, the wall closing shut behind it.

"Hopefully I've taught some people in town that villagers can be heroes too," said Ripley, "that's all I ever wanted: to inspire the next generation of villagers to be more adventurous than our parents were; to show them that they don't have to rely on Steve to save them. That statue the mayor built of me in the town center is a bit embarrassing, but it'll be worth it if it inspires a few baby villagers to grow up to be heroes. Now I want to go to new places—to teach villagers across the world what it means to be a hero."

Dave was inspired.

"Maybe you could come with us?" Dave said. "Imagine: two villagers defeating the ender dragon before Steve! How great would that be!"

"I was hoping you'd ask that," Ripley said. "I'd be

honored. As soon as I heard about your quest, I knew I had to join. Thank you, Dave."

Dave suddenly has a thought.

"Your mob spawner things," he said, "I don't suppose you can spawn endermen?"

It had suddenly struck him how much easier it would be to get ender eyes if they could just spawn and kill endermen in this room.

"Afraid not," said Ripley. "I don't have any endermen spawn eggs. How come?"

"Oh, no reason," said Dave.

Dave would have stayed the whole night in Ripley's training room if he could, but Ripley said they both ought to get some sleep—it was late after all.

By the time Dave got back to the inn, Carl and Porkins were already asleep. Dave climbed into his bed, his mind racing with exciting thoughts. He'd finally met another villager who thought like him: another villager who thought the world didn't have to revolve around Steve. And, best of all, Ripley had agreed to join them on their adventure!

When he finally got to sleep, Dave had a big smile on his face.

CHAPTER NINE

Zombie Attack!

At the mayor's request, Dave, Steve, Porkins and Carl agreed to stay in town a few more days.

"It's so nice to have guests," the mayor told them. "Especially adventurers!"

Dave got the impression that the mayor liked to keep popular people around him, like Steve and Ripley, to help his own popularity.

Dave spent most of the time in Ripley's basement, training. When Ripley had free time he'd teach Dave to sword fight, using Robo-Ripley as a sparring partner. Dave would spar with the robot as Ripley yelled advice at him.

"Keep your shoulders square!" Ripley would say. "Keep your guard up!"

For Dave it was also nice to be able to relax and not be on the road for a few days. He, Porkins and Carl were given all the best food and were treated to massages, hot baths and whatever else they desired.

"This is the life," said Carl, eating a baked potato as he, Dave and Porkins sat on a balcony overlooking the town. "Maybe we should just stay here and be treated like kings for the rest of our lives!"

"They're only treating us so well because we're friends with Steve," Dave said. Down below he could see the huge statues of Steve and Ripley in the town square.

Maybe one day people will build a statue of me, Dave thought. *When I've killed the ender dragon.*

Suddenly there were screams from below.

"Help!" Dave could hear people yelling. "Someone help!"

"Not again," Carl groaned. "Why are you villagers always in trouble?"

"Come on," Dave said. "Grab your swords—we have to help."

"Why?" Carl asked. "There are already two heroes in town—Ripley and Steve. Why do they need us?"

"He's got a point, old bean," said Porkins. "What can we do? Surely we'd just be in the way."

"Look," snapped Dave angrily, "we're meant to be heroes!"

"I thought we were adventurers?" said Carl.

"It's the same thing!" said Dave.

Carl and Porkins were both looking at him with

shocked expressions.

"I'm sorry," Dave said, trying to calm himself down. "I just want to help."

"Ok," said Carl, "let's go then, I guess. Porkins—you can carry me."

The three of them made their way towards the source of the commotion, running along down the narrow cobblestone streets.

"What's going on?" Dave asked a villager fleeing in the opposite direction.

"Zombies!" yelled the villager. "Zombies in the town!"

And he ran off.

Dave, Porkins and Carl kept going until they reached the big town square, where villagers were running from a horde of zombies.

"Look," said Porkins, "they're not normal zombies— they're zombie villagers!"

Porkins was right, Dave saw. The zombies chasing the villagers were zombie villagers—and every villager they caught turned into another zombie villager.

"Come on," Carl said, "get your swords out, let's get this over with."

"We can't kill them," Dave said, "they're villagers!"

Dave had no idea what to do. As far as he knew, the only thing that could cure zombie villagers was using the potion of weakness on them and then feeding them a golden apple, but he had neither of those things.

Suddenly Dave saw the mayor running across the square, his fat belly wobbling. Chasing him was a fat zombie villager Dave recognized as being the mayor's son.

"Heeeelp!" The mayor yelled. "My son is trying to eat me!"

"Wow," said Carl. "It sure is tough being a parent."

Suddenly a figure clad in diamond armor jumped down from the rooftops.

"I'll save you, Mr Mayor!" said the figure, raising its sword. It was Steve.

He ran towards the mayor's son, screaming a battle cry.

"IT'S STEVE TIME!!!!"

"No!" Dave yelled. "It's not a normal zombie!"

But Steve didn't hear him, he was too busy getting ready to swing his sword.

"Steve no!" said the mayor, looking on in horror. "That's my son!"

Suddenly Ripley ran forward, blocking Steve's diamond sword with his own. He was also clad in diamond armor.

"What are you doing, bro?" Steve said angrily. "I'm trying to stop the zombies!"

"Those are innocent people, you idiot!" said Ripley. "Zombie villagers!"

Steve's face fell.

"I... I didn't know, bro!"

"Idiot," snarled Ripley.

Ripley pulled out a bottle of blue potion and drank it. Suddenly he started moving at super speed, quickly building a structure in the middle of the town square.

That must have been some sort of speed potion, Dave thought.

Ripley finished building his contraption: it was a small rectangular structure made of dispensers. He flipped a switch on the side and all the dispensers started firing out hundreds of potion bottles.

"Take cover!" Ripley yelled to Dave and the others.

They quickly hid behind a bench, peering over to watch as the potion bottles from the machine flew through the air and smashed against the zombies, covering them with liquid.

"What is that potion?" The mayor asked.

"Splash potion of weakness," said Dave. "Look, the zombies are calming down!"

The zombies were no longer running around: instead they were slowly lurching from side to side, as if they might fall asleep at any moment.

"Right, phase two!" yelled Ripley. He flipped another switch, and the machine stopped firing out potions—and fired out golden apples instead.

"Wow!" said Dave.

The apples landed near the zombies or hit into them. When the zombies saw the apples they looked at them curiously, then picked them up and took a bite.

The golden apples were irresistible to zombies, it seemed, and soon all the zombies were munching down apple after apple.

"They're changing!" said the mayor excitedly. "They're changing back to normal!"

He was right—the green in the zombies' skin was beginning to fade, as they transformed back to normal villagers. They all seemed to be unharmed—if very confused.

"Where am I?" one of the zombies asked. Dave noticed it was Phillip, the villager they'd saved in the igloo. Phillip looked over and spotted Ripley and his machine. "Ripley! Ripley saved us!"

Soon everyone was rushing over to Ripley, hugging him and congratulating him.

"That dude is such a show off," said Steve to Dave, rolling his eyes. "Bro, I was killing bad guys when he was still in diapers!"

And with that, Steve slumped off.

"What's wrong with him?" Porkins asked.

"I think he's jealous," Dave said, unable to hide the happy grin on his face. "Jealous that, for once, he's not the biggest hero in town."

That night there was a big feast in Ripley's honor. Steve didn't even turn up this time. Dave went back to the inn to try and get Steve to come and join them, but Steve wasn't in his room.

"I think he's sulking somewhere," Dave told Porkins and Carl when he returned to the feast.

There was no sign of Steve all that night, but Dave was having too much fun to care. After a night of eating and celebrating, he went to bed with a full stomach and a smile on his face.

In his dreams that night he imagined a feast in his own honor: everyone chanting *Dave! Dave! Dave!* and telling him what a hero he was. His parents were there, and they were so proud of him.

"Dave!" he heard a voice say. "Dave wake up!"

He woke. Porkins was standing over him.

"There's something going on again, old chap," said Porkins nervously. "I heard yelling outside."

Suddenly the landlady burst through the door.

"Come quick!" she said. "Your friend Steve—he's threatening to blow up the town!"

CHAPTER TEN

Steve Turns to the Dark Side

Dave, Carl and Porkins ran as fast as they could towards the town center. When they got there, Steve was standing on the top of his golden statue, surrounded by a huge crowd of villagers.

"You bros had your chance to worship me as you should!" Steve was yelling. "But you chose to worship that idiot Ripley instead, and now you will all pay! I've filled the caves under your town with TNT, and I'm going to destroy it and build an even BIGGER statue of me in its place!"

The villagers started screaming and running. In typical villager-style, they were running around in circles and bumping into things and not doing a very good job of escaping.

"Steve!" Dave yelled. "This isn't you! I know you're angry, but this isn't the way!"

But Steve ignored him. He jumped off of the statue and quickly ran across the square, disappearing down a side street.

"We've got to stop him," Dave said to Porkins and Carl.

"But he's Steve," said Carl, "he's our friend. And besides, he'd whup our butts."

"I don't want a whupped butt," said Porkins. "That doesn't sound very nice."

"EVERYONE LISTEN!"

It was Ripley, standing on a rooftop.

"We need to evacuate the town, before it blows up! This way, to the north gate!"

The villagers stopped running around like idiots and began to head off in the direction Ripley was telling them to go. There were so many that there was a huge queue, everyone pushing and shoving to escape.

"Come on," said Carl, "let's get out of here."

"No," said Dave, "I have to stop Steve. He may be an idiot, but this isn't like him—blowing up an entire town."

"Um, didn't he blow up your entire village?" asked Carl.

"Well, yes," said Dave, "but that was out of stupidity—not malice. It's not like Steve to get angry, and I think if he does this he might never forgive himself."

"Dave!" Ripley yelled down at them from the rooftop. "You three have to get out of here!"

"I can't," Dave shouted back. "I'm sorry Ripley, I have to stop Steve."

Dave ran out of the square, with no real idea of where he was going.

Where could Steve be? he wondered.

Then he remembered what Steve had said—about filling the caves under the town with TNT—and he knew where he had to go. He ran to Ripley's house, opened the door, and slid down the ladder.

When he reached Ripley's basement, the hole in the floor was already open, and Dave could see the lava pool below. He peered over the edge and saw the lava was actually quite far below, in the middle of a huge cave. He also saw something that chilled his bones: the walls of the cave were all lined with hundreds of blocks of TNT—thankfully just out of reach of the lava.

"Steve!" Dave called down into the cave. "Steve, where are you?"

"Over here, little bro!"

It was Steve, but his voice wasn't coming from the cave, it was coming from the room Dave was in—Ripley's basement.

Dave looked up and saw Steve at the side of the room, trapped in a cage made of iron bars.

"Help me, bro!" Steve yelled.

Dave was confused.

"Steve, what's going on? Five minutes ago you were threatening to blow up the town."

"Bro that wasn't me," said Steve.

"No it wasn't," said a voice from behind Dave. "For once, Steve is innocent."

Dave turned round.

It was Ripley.

CHAPTER ELEVEN
Ripley's Plan

Ripley was standing at the foot of the ladder. On his left side was a villager who looked exactly like him (*Robo-Ripley*, Dave realized) and on his right was an identical copy of Steve.

"You've already met Robo-Ripley," said Ripley, "so meet Robo-Steve."

"It was you!" Dave gasped. "Your robot was the one who threatened to blow up the town, not Steve!"

Ripley smiled.

"I should thank you, Dave," he said. "You gave me the idea when you told me about Steve blowing up your village. I could use my robot to frame Steve, and ruin his name forever. I'd already made my name as a hero by releasing monsters into the town for me to defeat, but my victory won't be complete until villagers across the world all hate the name *Steve*."

"All those monsters.... that was you?" said Dave.

"Of course," said Ripley. "I summoned the wither, I created the zombie outbreak, and plenty more before that. I planned it carefully, of course, so no-one ever got hurt."

"I bet you were the one running zombie experiments in that igloo as well," said Dave.

"Guilty," said Ripley. "I needed to make sure the cure worked before unleashing zombies on the town."

"That's not cool, bro," said Steve. "Not cool at all."

"Why?" said Dave to Ripley. "Why are you doing this?"

"Dave, I thought you of all people would understand," said Ripley sadly. "For too long our people have been held back by our love for Steve. After Snow Town is destroyed, villagers around the world will realize they were wrong about Steve. He's not a hero, he's a villain."

"No he's not!" snapped Dave. "He may be an idiot, he may do stupid things, but when it comes to the crunch he does the right thing. Well, most of the time."

"I'm disappointed," said Ripley. "I like you Dave. I would have come with you on your quest to kill the ender dragon. We could have both gone down in history as villager heroes, but now I'm going to have to kill you. I can't have my secret getting out."

He turned to the robots.

"Kill mode activated," he told them. "And Robo-Steve, once all the villagers have evacuated I want you to activate the TNT and blow up the town. Is that clear?"

"Blow up the town once the villagers are clear," said Robo-Steve, his voice sounding exactly like Steve's. "Affirmative, bro."

"I programmed him to say *bro* a lot," Ripley grinned. "I thought it was the best way to make him sound like the real Steve."

Ripley began to climb back up the ladder as the robots drew their swords.

"I'm sorry Dave," Ripley called from the ladder. "I wish things could have worked out differently."

"I wish your face could have worked out differently!" Dave shouted back.

Ripley shook his head. "Maybe you're more like Steve than I realized. Goodbye Dave."

Dave drew his sword. Both robots—Robo-Steve and Robo-Ripley—we're closing in on him. There was no way he could take them both on.

I'm a hero, he thought, *I can do this!*

No you can't, said another voice in his head. *Even a hero needs friends.*

He knew what he had to do.

Dave turned and ran in the opposite direction. He could hear the robots start to chase him as he pulled out a diamond pickaxe and rushed towards Steve's cage. He raised the pickaxe and swung it at the bars, cutting through them as fast as could.

"Come on little bro!" Steve yelled. "You can do it!"

Dave looked behind and saw the robots were nearly on him. He swung a final pickaxe blow and suddenly the bars shattered.

"Give me your sword!" said Steve.

Dave threw his sword to Steve. Steve jumped through the broken bars, swinging the sword just in time to block a sword thrust from Robo-Ripley.

As Steve fought off the two robots, Dave ran to the weapons rack to grab another sword. This one was only iron, but it was the only one he could find. He quickly spun around just in time to block a blow from Robo-Steve.

"I've seen you fight, bro," said Robo-Steve. "Fighting me is pointless—your skill level isn't high enough."

"Good job I'm not fighting alone then," said Dave.

Robo-Steve turned round just in time to see Steve swing his sword down, burying the blade in the robot's head.

"*ERROR!*" the robot said, his voice sounding robotic now. "*CRITICAL ERROR!*"

Robo-Steve collapsed to the floor. The other robot, Robo-Ripley, came running at them, but Steve quickly swung round and kicked it in the chest. The robot staggered backwards, tottering on the edge of the pit that opened up above the lava lake.

"*Extreme danger detected!*" said Robo Ripley—then it fell backwards, down through the cave and into the lava.

"Nice one Steve," said Dave.

"I couldn't have done it without you freeing me from the cage, bro," said Steve. "So I guess you deserve some credit too."

"Come on," Dave said. "Once Ripley realizes his robots are out of action he'll set the explosives off himself. We have to stop him."

The two of them ran towards the ladder, climbing up it as fast as they could.

When they reached the town square, a few villagers were still trying to push their way out down the narrow streets.

"Come on!" Ripley was yelling at them. "You have to evacuate!"

Then Ripley spotted Dave and Steve and the color drained from his face.

"Traitors!" Ripley yelled. "Look everyone, it's the traitor Steve, and he's working with Dave!"

Before Dave could protest, something flew through the air and landed in the middle of the square.

"Oh no," said Dave, "it's still alive!"

It was Robo-Steve. It had a huge cut in the middle of its face from where Steve had hit it with his sword, but it was very much alive.

"*Error overridden,*" said Robo-Steve. "*Mission resumed. Blow up town.*"

The villagers had stopped evacuating to stare at what was going on.

"That's a robot Steve!" one of them said. "Cool!"

"Get out of here!" Ripley snapped at the villagers. "Now!"

The villagers all started to push and shove again, trying desperately to escape the square and the town.

"*Searching memory banks for location of TNT switch,*" said Robo-Steve. "*Must blow up the town.*"

"No!" said Ripley. "You're meant to blow up the town after everyone has evacuated!"

"*Blow up town,*" repeated Robo-Steve.

"Robo-Steve, deactivate!" yelled Ripley.

"*Error, deactivation program corrupted. Cannot deactivate. Blow up the town! Blow up the town!*"

Robo-Steve looked up at the rooftops, suddenly spotting the thing he was looking for.

"*TNT switch location found.*"

Dave followed the robot's gaze and saw that, yes, a switch had been stuck to the roof of one of the buildings.

Ripley must have created a redstone trail from that switch to the TNT, Dave thought.

"No!" Ripley yelled, but the robot ignored him. It did a superhuman jump into the air, landing on the roof next to the switch.

"*Blow up the town,*" the robot repeated, grabbing hold of the switch.

"Blow this up, you rascal!"

It was Porkins. He and Carl had come running back into the town square. Porkins was aiming his bow at Robo-Steve. He fired and the arrow struck true, hitting the robot in the back.

"*ERROR!*" screamed the robot, "*ERROR!*"

It let go of the switch and stumbled backwards, falling off the roof. It landing with a *thud* on the cobblestone ground.

"Well," said Carl, "I'm glad that's all over."

But he'd spoken too soon. Robo-Steve staggered to its feet. Half of its fake skin had torn off, allowing them to see the metal body underneath. One of its robotic eyes had been revealed, and it glowed red.

Blow up town," the robot said. "*Blow up town!*"

"You idiot robot," said Ripley. "Not until everyone is evacuated!"

Ripley charged at the robot with a diamond sword, but Robo-Steve was too quick for him. It drew its own diamond sword and stabbed Ripley through the chest.

"Ripley!" yelled Dave.

Ripley fell to the floor.

The robot turned to face Dave. Steve, Carl and Porkins all stepped forward, their swords raised.

"Looks like you're outnumbered, bro," said Steve.

"*Probability of success thirty-three-per-cent,*" said Robo-Steve. "*More power needed. Accessing emergency building supplies.*"

Robo-Steve's chest opened and inside Dave could see a collection of tiny blocks and tools. Robo-Steve pulled out a diamond pickaxe. It ran towards the gold Steve statue in the middle of the square and dug its way through the gold blocks, disappearing into the statue's leg.

"What's it doing?" said Dave. "Hiding in the statue?"

"Oh no," said Ripley.

Dave had forgotten about Ripley: he was on the floor, clutching the wound on his chest. Dave ran over to him.

"It's ok," Dave said, "we'll get you some healing potion."

"No," said Ripley. "We have to stop the robot! It must be using the redstone supplies I gave it."

"Using the redstone for what?" asked Dave.

Suddenly there was a tremendous noise of scraping metal and breaking cobblestone. Dave looked around and saw one of the most terrifying sights he'd ever seen in his life.

The giant golden Steve statue had come to life...

CHAPTER TWELVE

Statue Fight

"Oh my!" said Porkins. "This doesn't look good, chaps!"

"It's Robo-Steve," said Ripley, "he's controlling the statue from the inside using redstone."

The huge gold statue stumbled towards them, each footstep shaking the ground. It was getting used to walking, each step taking a long time.

"Do you have any redstone?" Ripley asked Dave.

Dave shook his head.

"I've got some bro," said Steve.

Ripley gave Steve a look of pure hatred.

"Fine!" he snapped. "Give me everything redstone-related you have—including any switches, buttons and repeaters. Quickly!"

Steve took off his bag and quickly handed all his redstone to Ripley.

"Now get me inside the other statue!" roared Ripley.

"Are you sure about this?" said Dave. "You're hurt, you

need help."

"This is all my fault," said Ripley. "I was so focused on my hatred for Steve that I put the whole town in danger. I need to put a stop to this."

Dave took out his pickaxe and started hacking away at a diamond block at the foot of the giant diamond Ripley statue.

"Hurry!" said Ripley. "We're running out of time!"

He was right. The gold Steve statue was getting used to walking now, taking more confident steps. It was nearly upon them.

"Come on guys," Steve said. "I may be the greatest warrior who ever lived, but even I might have trouble fighting a statue!"

The diamond block broke and Ripley crawled inside the diamond villager statue.

"Get everyone out of the town!" Ripley yelled to Dave. "I'll hold Robo-Steve off as long as I can."

"Good luck, Ripley," Dave said.

"Go!" Ripley roared.

"Come on," Dave said to the others, "time to go!"

Dave and his friends ran out of the square and down a side street. Up ahead they saw some villagers, still pushing and shoving each other to get out of the town.

"Haven't villagers ever heard of queuing?" Porkins

said. "No wonder it's taking them so long to evacuate—they keep pushing each other!"

"Maybe they just need to push a bit harder then," said Dave. "Carl, do you mind?"

Dave picked up Carl.

"Hey!" said Carl angrily. "What are you playing at?"

Dave ran forward, holding Carl out in front of him.

"Help!" Dave yelled. "This creeper is going to explode!"

The villagers started screaming and pushing to get away.

"A creeper!"

"Let me through! Let me through!"

Before long all the villagers had pushed their way out of the town. Dave and his friends followed them.

The villagers had gathered a short way up the mountain, on a cliff overlooking the town. They were all staring intently at something going on in the town, and Dave knew exactly what it must be.

Dave pushed through the crowd and peered over the edge of the cliff. Below, in the town square, the two giant statues were fighting: the gold Steve statue, controlled by Robo-Steve, and the diamond villager statue, controlled by Ripley. The huge statues were slashing at each other with their swords, each mighty blow shaking the mountain.

The statues had already left a trail of broken buildings

in their wake, and Dave knew it wouldn't be long before they disturbed the TNT underneath the town.

"Everyone keep moving!" Dave yelled. "We have to get as far from the town as possible!"

But before he could get the villagers to move any further, there was a mighty explosion: *DOOM BOOM BOOM BOOM DOOOOM!!!!*

Blocks flew threw the air and Dave had to clutch his ears to block out the sound.

When the explosion finally stopped, Snow Town was gone. All that was left were a few half-destroyed buildings and a crater with a lake of lava at the bottom.

At least we got the villagers out, Dave thought. *Apart from poor Ripley.*

"My town!" said the mayor, falling to his knees. "My beautiful town!"

Most of the villagers were in tears now: the only home they had ever known was completely destroyed. Dave knew how they felt.

"I know this is bad, but you can build a new town," Dave told them. "A better town than before."

The mayor pointed at Steve.

"You!" he said. "You did this!"

"It wasn't Steve," said one of the villagers sadly. "It was Ripley. He had a Steve robot, I saw." It was Phillip, Dave realized: the villager they'd rescued from the igloo.

The one who'd been such a big Ripley fan.

His wife Liz went up to him, but instead of having a go at him she put her arms around his waist.

"At least everyone's safe," Porkins said to Dave. "You did a ruddy good job, old bean."

"Yeah, I guess you're more of a hero than I thought," added Carl. "You're an idiot, but also a bit of a hero."

"Thanks," smiled Dave. Coming from Carl, that was a compliment.

Steve came over to Dave as well.

"Well done bro," he said. "You did well back there— that was quick thinking using the little creeper dude. Maybe one day you'll be as big a hero as me!"

"Thanks," smiled Dave.

Suddenly something fell from the sky, landing with a *thud* between Steve and Dave. The creature raised its metal head, its eyes glowing red.

It was Robo-Steve.

CHAPTER THIRTEEN
Robo-Steve's Last Stand

All the fake Steve skin and clothes had peeled off, and now Robo-Steve was nothing but metal. Somehow it still had its diamond sword.

"*Destroy town,*" it said, looking at the terrified villagers. "*Destroy! Destroy! Destroy!*"

"Not on our watch," said Steve. "Come on Dave, let's show this rust bucket who's boss.

Dave and Steve raised their swords.

"Let's do this, bro," said Dave, smiling.

"Hey!" said Steve, with a grin. "That's my word!"

The robot ran at them, swinging its sword wildly. Dave blocked the first blow, the diamond of the robot's sword clanging against the iron of his.

Steve swung his sword at the robot's back, but it was too quick, jumping out of the way so quickly that Steve's blow nearly cut Dave in half.

The robot swung his sword upwards but Steve quickly

blocked the hit, his diamond sword clashing with the robot's.

"*Destroy!*" the robot hissed. "*Destroy destroy DESTROY!!*"

"Come on Dave and Steve!" Dave heard Carl yell. "Kick that robot's butt!"

Dave looked round. Porkins, Carl, the mayor and the whole town were watching the fight, the villagers all cheering them on. He'd been so engrossed in the fight that he hadn't noticed.

"A little help here, bro!" Steve yelled.

Steve was fighting off a furious flurry of sword blows from Robo-Steve, the robot's hand moving so fast that it was hard to see.

Dave ran forward and swung his sword at the robot's back, but it was too quick, and brought its own sword round to block the blow.

"*You two are no match for my superior skill,*" the robot hissed.

Suddenly an arrow pierced the robot's right eye. The robot stumbled backwards, strange metallic noises coming from its mouth.

Dave turned round. Porkins was holding his bow, getting another arrow ready.

"You may be strong, old chap," said Porkins to the robot, "but we fight as a team."

Robo-Steve pulled the arrow from its eye and ran towards Porkins with its sword, ready to strike him down, but suddenly it tripped—over something small and green on the floor.

"Sorry buddy," Carl said, as the robot clattered across the ground, "I didn't see you there."

"*DESTROY!!!*" Robo-Steve screamed jumping to its feet. It tried to swing its sword at Carl, but Porkins fired another arrow at its head, striking its other eye.

The robot staggered backwards.

"*ERROR! FATAL ERROR! ACTIVATING EMERGENCY TELEPORT!*"

The robot's body started to hum, then there was a flash of purple and it disappeared.

"Is it gone?" Porkins asked.

The villagers all cheered, running forward and lifting Dave and his friends into the air.

"Well they certainly think it is," said Carl. "And if it comes back, we'll whup its butt again."

CHAPTER FOURTEEN
Goodbye Again

Steve built a big house for the villagers with his remaining materials. It was a bit cramped—with all the beds packed tightly together over three floors, but it would do until the villagers rebuilt their town.

"Thank you, you four, for all you've done for us," the mayor said, as he and the other villagers went to see Dave, Steve, Porkins and Carl off. The four of them had all been given new horses.

"I still can't believe Ripley tricked us," the mayor said angrily. "He made fools of us all."

"He changed his ways at the end though," said Dave. He didn't know why he felt the need to defend Ripley, after Ripley had nearly killed them all, but he did.

So Dave and the others said their goodbyes, then rode off, leaving the people of Snow Town behind.

They rode on until night, when they finally reached the end of the snow biome. Dave was overjoyed to finally see grass again.

Dave built them a small house to shelter in with some nether brick he had left over. They all went to sleep pretty quickly, but halfway through the night Dave was woken up by someone moving around.

"Who's there?" he called into the darkness.

"It's just me, little bro," Steve whispered.

Steve and Dave went outside. Steve had his backpack on.

"So you're leaving?" Dave asked.

"Yeah bro," said Steve. "This has been fun, but I'm more of a lone traveler. Besides, I've still gotta beat you to that dragon!"

Dave grinned.

"The race is on," he said. Then, reluctantly, he added: "Steve, do you want me to tell you how to make eyes of ender?" You won't get very far in finding an ender portal without them.

"Nah," said Steve, "I'll work it out. Or I'll randomly stumble into one. You know me."

"You probably will," said Dave with a smile.

"Right," said Steve. "I, uh, guess this is it, bro."

The two of them had an awkward hug, then Steve climbed up on his horse.

"Keep it Stevey," said Steve, giving Dave a salute.

"Good luck," Dave said.

Steve grinned. "Bro, when you're as good as me, you don't need luck."

With that, Steve pulled on the horse's reigns and galloped away. Dave watched him go, until he disappeared behind some trees.

"Where's Steve?" asked Carl, sticking his head out of the house.

"He's gone," said Dave. "You know how heroes are. They love working alone."

"Fair enough," said Carl. "So what now?"

"Now, Dave said, a smile on his face, "we go endermen hunting."

"I wish I hadn't asked," said Carl.

CHAPTER FIFTEEN

Return to the Nether

Porkins crept towards the zombie pigman, as Dave and Carl watched from behind a block.

Dave never thought he'd be back in the Nether so soon, but here he was. After their adventure in the snow, Porkins was understandably anxious to find out if golden apples could cure zombie pigmen the same way they cured zombies.

The zombie pigman looked at Porkins curiously. The two of them were both pigmen, but the zombie pigmen had been corrupted, turned into mindless beasts by the mysterious Herobrine. As far as Porkins knew, he was the last pigman who *hadn't* been turned into a zombie.

Porkins slowly pulled out a bottle from his backpack, taking his time so he didn't frighten the zombie. Zombie pigmen were normally fairly calm—unless they thought they were under attack.

"This is the tricky part," Dave whispered to Carl. "He's

got to splash the zombie with the potion, but if it thinks it's being attacked it'll attack back—and all its friends will join in too."

"Thanks for the running commentary," said Carl, rolling his eyes. Before he met Carl, Dave wouldn't have thought it was *possible* for a Creeper to roll its eyes, but somehow Carl did it all the time.

Porkins edged forward. He was barely a block away from the zombie pigman now. He uncorked the potion... then jerked the bottle forward, covering the zombie pigman in liquid.

"SQUEEE!!!"

The zombie pigman flapped its arms and squinted its eyes. All the other zombie pigman turned to watch, and for a second it looked like they all might attack, but then the potion-covered pigman relaxed again.

"The potion is weakening him, calming him down," Dave whispered.

"Enough with the commentary!" said Carl.

Porkins reached into his backpack and pulled out a golden apple, then held it out in front of him, offering it to the zombie pigman.

"Here you go, old chap," said Porkins. "A delicious apple, all for you!"

The zombie pigman looked at the apple suspiciously. For a second it looked as if it was going to turn and walk away, but then it snatched the apple out of Porkins's trotter and started stuffing it into its mouth.

In a few big bites, the apple was gone. The zombie pigman burped loudly.

"Charming," said Carl.

Porkins walked over to Dave and Carl, joining them behind their rock.

"And now we wait!" he said excitedly. And wait they did. They waited and waited and waited, but the zombie pigman just kept shuffling around like a zombie.

Eventually Porkins went back over to it.

"Can... you... understand... what... I'm... saying... old... chap?" Porkins asked. The zombie pigman looked at him blankly.

They tried the process with five more zombie pigmen —spraying them with Splash Potion of Weakness and then feeding them a golden apple—but each time it seemed to make no difference.

"Blast it all," said Porkins sadly. "I really thought it would work."

Finally Porkins admitted defeat, and the three of them headed back to their nether portal. When they emerged on the other side it was the middle of the day, the sun shining brightly overhead.

Dave had built the portal in the middle of a vast plain biome. There was grass in every direction.

"Maybe we should just stay here," said Carl. "Build ourselves a nice house, spend every day lying in the sun. It would make a nice change from running for our lives."

Dave grinned. "You're welcome to stay if you want," he told the creeper. "I'll even build you a house. We could put up a statue of you outside, made of green wool."

"No thanks," said Carl, "I've had enough of statues to last me a lifetime."

"Talking of houses, we should build ourselves one," said Porkins. "The sun will be going down soon, chaps."

So Dave and Porkins built a basic wooden house, while Carl relaxed in the sun. It wasn't much, but it had three beds and would protect them from hostile mobs.

"I thought you were meant to be hunting Endermen?" said Carl to Dave as they all climbed into their beds.

Carl was right. Dave had all the blaze rods he needed, after their adventure in the Nether, and now he needed ender pearls—and the only way to get those, according to his books, was to kill endermen. Only with both the pearls and the rods could he make eyes of ender—the magical trinkets that showed the way to ender portals.

"Tomorrow," Dave said. "We'll start tomorrow."

It started raining outside. Occasionally Dave could hear a strange wheezing sound, like a creature in pain.

"Those are endermen," said Carl. They don't like the rain so they keep teleporting to escape."

Dave looked out of the window. Occasionally he saw strange dark creatures appearing then disappearing.

"Sometimes after storms you find a few ender pearls on the ground," said Carl, "from endermen who got killed by the rain."

"So water kills them?" asked Dave.

"Yup," said Carl. "You never know, you might get lucky—if enough endermen get killed tonight, we could end up with all the pearls we need."

After the long day they'd had, Dave soon found himself falling asleep. In his dreams he was a fierce knight in diamond armor, fighting a dragon.

When he woke, it was still dark. In the dark he could hear something making a strange noise.

His heart stopped. He knew what that noise was.

He opened his eyes slowly, looking down at the floor. As his eyes adjusted to the moonlight he saw two thin, long, black sticks. *No*, he thought, *not sticks—legs*.

An enderman was inside their house.

CHAPTER SIXTEEN
Dave vs Enderman

Dave's first instinct was to look up at the enderman, but he quickly remembered what a bad idea that would be. He'd never seen an enderman in person before, but he knew from the books he'd read and the scary stories he'd been told as a child that if you looked at one in the eye, it would attack you.

The enderman made some more strange noises and started walking slowly around the tiny house. Dave watched as it leaned down and pulled up one of the cobblestone blocks from the floor.

Dave looked across the room at the two other beds. Thankfully Porkins and Carl were still asleep.

What do I do? he thought desperately. *What do I do?*

His bed was next to the door, so if he was careful he could probably get out and shut the door behind him before being caught—but that would just leave Porkins and Carl alone with the enderman.

The house was only small with one room, and the enderman was standing right in the middle of the floor, so there was no way he could wake Porkins and Carl and sneak them out. No, he only had one choice: he was going to have to kill the enderman.

Dave had no idea how easy or difficult it was to kill an enderman, but he had a diamond sword and knew how to use it. The only trouble was, his rucksack was on the other side of the room.

The enderman dropped the cobblestone block, then leaned down to pick up another one. Seeing that this might be his only chance, Dave slowly climbed out of bed, trying hard not to make any noise.

"Potatoes..."

It was Carl, talking in his sleep. The enderman made a curious noise, turning its head to look at Carl.

Please don't wake up, Carl, Dave thought. With the enderman distracted, Dave crawled across the floor towards his bag.

"Baked potatoes..." muttered Carl.

Dave finally reached his bag. Being as quiet as he could, he slowly opened the zip. Then he slipped his hand inside, feeling around for his sword. A jolt of pain rushed through him and he pulled his hand out of the bag. Blood was running down his arm—he'd cut a finger on the blade of his sword. Dave put the finger in his mouth, sucking it and trying his best not to make a sound.

"What's going on?" muttered Carl. "Who's making those weird noises?" Dave watched in horror as Carl opened his eyes, looking right at the enderman.

"Arrrgggghh!!!" said Carl.

The enderman screamed, a long, horrible, sound that hurt Dave's ears, its mouth opening wide.

Dave reached into his bag again, grabbing the hilt of his sword, ignoring the pain in his finger.

"Heeeelp!" yelled Carl.

The enderman ran forward towards Carl, still making the horrible screaming sound. Dave swung his sword at the creature's legs. The enderman screamed in pain then turned to face Dave, screaming in his face.

It was Dave's first proper look at it. The enderman was a tall, thin creature, with jet black skin and soulless pink eyes. When it opened its mouth he could see through the back of its head.

The creature rushed at Dave, who quickly swung his sword, burying the blade between the creature's eyes. With one final, horrible scream it fell to the floor, then *poof* it was gone.

Carl was breathing rapidly, terror still in his eyes.

"You ok?" Dave asked him.

"Not really," Carl replied.

The creeper jumped out of bed. He leaned down and

picked up a tiny green ball. *An ender pearl*, thought Dave, recognizing it from his crafting book.

"One down," said Carl. "And all it took to get it, was me almost getting killed."

There was a grunting from across the room. Porkins was snoring.

"And he slept through it all," said Carl to Dave. "Typical."

CHAPTER SEVENTEEN

The Ender Hunters

In the morning, Dave, Carl and Porkins went outside. As Carl had suspected, there were some ender pearls left on the ground, from endermen who had been killed by the rain. There were only three though, leaving Dave with a grand total of four pearls.

"Well, it's a start," said Dave. "Now, let's make an eye of ender."

According to the old book Dave had found in the stronghold under his village, using eyes of ender was the only way to find ender portals. All you had to do was throw them into the sky and they would show you which direction to go.

Dave took a blaze rod and an ender pearl and held them next to each other. With a *pop* both the pearl and rod disappeared, and in their place was a strange green eye.

"Yes!" said Dave. "It worked!"

"Did you think it wouldn't?" asked Carl.

"After all the things we've been through, nothing would surprise me," said Dave. "But the good news is that now we have a way of finding the End. We can finally go and fight the ender dragon!"

"Oh I'm so happy," said Carl, who didn't sound very happy at all.

"I think it's splendid news, old bean!" said Porkins. "So what do you have to do with that eye thing?"

"This," said Dave. He threw the eye of ender into the air. It hovered in place for a moment, then flew off across the sky.

"That's the direction we have to go," said Dave. He looked up at the sky. "Judging from the position of the sun, that's south west—so let's keep heading south west. We don't want to have to use more ender eyes than we need to, we've only got three pearls left."

So off they went, following the route the ender eye had taken. Soon they found themselves walking near to a little village, nestled at the foot of a mountain.

"Shall we go and check it out?" Dave asked the other two. "It might be nice to sleep in a proper inn and have a good meal."

"I dunno," said Carl, "the last time we stopped at a town we nearly got killed by giant statues and blown to bits by TNT."

"They might have baked potatoes," said Dave.

Carl's face lit up. He'd run out of potatoes a while back, and Dave knew he was desperate to have more of his favorite food.

"Alright," said Carl. "Although I know I'll regret this."

There were only five buildings in the whole village, but the inn was fairly busy nonetheless, with lots of villagers eating, drinking and chatting.

"We get a lot of visitors here in Little Orchid," the landlady told them, "travelers always stop here before crossing the mountains. We even had the famous Steve stop here once!"

"Never heard of him," said Dave.

There were no rooms free, but the landlady let them sleep in the stable with the horses. Dave set up the three beds he always kept in his backpack, and the three of them settled down to get to sleep.

"What's the point of staying the night with a bunch of smelly horses when we could just build a house of our own?" said Carl.

"I don't think they're smelly," said Porkins, who was quite fond of the horses. He leaned out of his bed and rubbed one of the horses' noses. "You're not smelly, are you dear chap?"

"Now you're gonna smell of horse too," said Carl.

At breakfast the next day, Dave went over to the landlady for a chat.

"Are there any areas around here where there are a lot of endermen?" he asked her.

The landlady shivered.

"Why would you want to go near endermen?" she asked. "You're not one of those Ender Hunters, are you?"

"Ender Hunters?" said Dave.

The landlady nodded at some villagers sitting in the far corner of the inn. They were wearing cowboy hats.

"Ender Hunters," she said. "They go hunting for endermen so they can sell the pearls. It's a dangerous job, make no mistake."

Dave's eyes lit up. If these *Ender Hunters* sold ender pearls, maybe he, Porkins and Carl wouldn't even need to hunt any more endermen themselves.

Dave went over to the Ender Hunters. There were four of them, and as Dave came up to them they gave him a suspicious look.

"What can we do for ya, partner?" one of them asked Dave. He was a short villager with a black beard. Dave had never seen a villager with a beard before.

"I hear you sell ender pearls," said Dave. "Can I buy some?"

The ender hunters all laughed.

"Ok, little man" the short villager said. "If you've got the money, we can sort you out. It's a thousand emeralds for one pearl. But we can do you a special deal—two thousand emeralds for two."

"A thousand emeralds!" said Dave, shocked.

"Or two thousand for two," said the short villager, grinning.

"That's the same price!" said Dave.

The short villager thought for a moment.

"Oh yeah," he said. "I guess it is."

"How can it possibly be that much?" said Dave. "Who could afford that?!"

"We normally sell to the rich folk up in Diamond City," said another of the ender hunters—a fat villager with a tiny hat. "Theys got more money than sense, them folk. They like to wear the pearls as jewelery, or just use them as ornaments in their fancy houses."

"There's no way you could do me a deal?" asked Dave.

"How much you got?" asked the short villager.

"Um," Dave rummaged around in his bag, "seven emeralds."

The villagers all laughed.

"I tell you what," said the short villager, "I know a way you could get all the ender pearls you want."

"You do?" said Dave excitedly. "What is it?"

Five minutes later, Dave came back and joined Porkins and Carl at their table.

"What was that all about?" asked Carl. "Why were you speaking with those weirdos?"

"Um, I've got some good news," said Dave. "I've signed us all up to be Ender Hunters!"

"What the heck is an Ender Hunter?" asked Carl.

CHAPTER EIGHTEEN

Hunting Trip

"Pleased to meet y'all," said the short villager to Porkins and Carl. They were gathered outside, by the stable. "I'm Biff, the leader of our little group." He pointed at the fat villager. "This here is Boff, my deputy, and those other two are Boof and Bop."

"So your names are Biff, Boff, Boof and Bop?" said Carl.

"That's correct," said Biff.

"Doesn't that get confusing?"

"No, sir."

"Riiiiight," said Carl.

The Ender Hunters only had two spare horses, so Porkins took one and Dave shared the other with Carl.

"I don't think you'd be able to ride too well with them tiny little legs, anyway," Boff said to Carl.

"Whatever you say, Boof," said Carl.

"I'm Boff," said Boff.

"What a minute," said Boof, "I thought I was Boff."

"No," said Bop, "you're Bop."

Carl rolled his eyes. "Let's just get moving, shall we," he said.

So off they went. Biff led the way, the others following behind, as the horses rode down a path between the mountains. Dave had never ridden a horse before, but he soon got used to it, using his legs and the stirrups to control the direction the horse was traveling. There wasn't a cloud in the sky, the sun beating down on them from overhead.

They stopped for the night by some trees.

"Shall I build us a house?" said Dave.

Biff scoffed.

"A house! Why, you three really are city folk, ain't you?"

"I'm from a village," said Dave.

"I'm from the Nether," said Porkins.

"I was born deep underground, where there's no light or fresh air, and every day is a struggle for survival," said Carl.

"Yup," said Biff. "A bunch of city boys. Real men, like us, sleep under the stars."

"Aren't you worried about mobs attacking you in the night?" said Dave.

"Nah," said Biff. "Our old leader, Bogg, used to worry about that, but not me."

"What happened to him?" asked Poker.

"He was slain by mobs in the night," said Biff.

So they all slept under a tree. Dave found it hard to get to sleep without the protection of a roof over his head and the comfort of a bed, but somehow he managed it.

In the morning they set off again. They rode through the mountains until, around lunchtime, the mountains ended and they saw a huge desert biome stretching out before them.

"Wow," said Dave, who had never seen a desert before. "It's so... yellow."

"Desert biomes is the best place ta hunt endermen," said Biff. "Big, open plains with nowhere for the varmints to hide. We'll set up a base, and wait for nightfall. You three all have swords, right?"

"Yep," said Dave.

"Good," said Biff. "Remember the deal—you get to keep half of all the pearls you get. The other half goes to me and my men."

The four Ender Hunters built a sandstone hut in the middle of a wide expanse of desert. Flat plains of sand stretched off into the distance in every direction.

"This here is the home base," said Biff. If you get

injured or need a place to rest, come back here. I'll fill a chest full of cooked chicken and fish.

"So what's the plan, then?" asked Carl. "Are you just gonna run around with you swords killing endermen all night?"

"That's right," grinned Biff. "What's tha matter, little creeper—you scared?"

"Well, yes," said Carl. "Isn't there some way we can trap them? Something we can build?"

"You city folk and your fancy ideas!" grinned Boff, the fat Ender Hunter. "Bock always used to say that too. *Isn't there any way we can trap the endermen? Any way we can farm them?*" He laughed. "Hunting them down with a sword is perfectly safe."

"What happened to Bock?" asked Porkins.

"He was slain by endermen," said Boff.

They spent the rest of the afternoon in the hut. The sun was so bright overhead that Biff said they should stay in the shade, to avoid getting sunstroke.

"I dunno why you worry about sunstroke," said Boff. "You sound just like Boop."

"What happened to Boop?" asked Porkins.

"Let me guess," said Carl. "He died of sunstroke?"

"No," said Boff, "he retired to spend more time with his wife."

"Oh," said Carl.

Eventually the sun began to set. "Time to get ready boys," Biff told them.

They all equipped themselves in armor. All of the Ender Hunters had gold armor. Dave had his diamond armor, Porkins stuck with his leather armor, and Carl didn't put any armor on at all.

"I'll stay and look after the base," he said. "It's a very important job."

Dave was about to put his diamond helmet on when Biff put a hand on his arm.

"No, partner," he said, "we wear these." And he handed Dave a tiny orange block. Dave turned the block over in his hands and saw a face on it.

"It's a pumpkin with a face carved into it?" he said, feeling confused.

"A carved pumpkin," said Biff. "Endermen attack when you look at them, but with one of these on your head, they won't even *know* you're looking at them."

"Nice," said Dave. The pumpkin grew to full size in his hands, then he equipped it on his head.

"It's hard to see out of though," he said.

Biff chuckled. "You'll get used to it. This way you can attack one enderman at a time, without accidentally looking at all his buddies and have them attack you too."

When it was finally dark, Dave, Porkins and the four Ender Hunters went outside. Biff laid a few torches down so they could see a bit, but mostly they were surrounded by darkness—the only light coming from the moon.

Porkins pulled out his bow.

"Fraid that won't do you much good, piggy," Biff said. "Endermen can see arrows coming—they teleport out of the way."

"Ah," said Porkins, sounding a bit worried. Dave knew that Porkins preferred to use his bow when he could. He wasn't a fan of hand-to-hand combat. Porkins pulled out a diamond sword instead, and switched his leather armor for diamond.

"Right," said Biff, "everyone wearing your pumpkin?" They all were.

"Then let's go!"

CHAPTER NINETEEN
Pearls and Rods

As Dave ran towards the darkness, sword in hand, he could barely see anything in front him. The combination of the pumpkin on his head and the lack of light made it very difficult to see where he was going, but he could just about make out some pink dots in the distance.

Enderman eyes.

Suddenly the endermen came into view, lit by the moonlight. There were about five of them, and they looked at Dave curiously. Nearby, hidden in the darkness, Dave could hear yells and enderman cries as the Ender Hunters and Porkins fought other endermen.

"Take that you dastardly cad!" he heard Porkins yell.

Endermen, it seemed, were unlike zombie pigmen—they didn't all swarm over when one of them was attacked.

Dave pulled out his sword.

"Yaaaa!" he yelled, running at one of the endermen. He slashed at it with his sword, and suddenly a transformation took place: the enderman opened its mouth and screamed, charging at Dave with its long, dark limbs.

"Oh crumbs," said Dave. He swung his sword again, forcing the enderman back. It kept coming and coming, moving at incredible speed, as Dave forced it back with sword blow after sword blow. Finally, with one final, ear-splitting scream, the enderman was slain, falling to the floor and disappearing with a *poof*. Dave picked up the ender pearl it dropped, putting it in his rucksack. The remaining endermen were looking at him curiously, as if nothing had happened.

Dave spent the rest of the night slaying enderman after enderman. By the time the sun started coming up, he'd got around fifteen pearls, to add to the four he already had.

"Come on," said Biff, coming over to him, "the night's over, that's enough hunting."

They spent the next five days out in the desert. During the day they'd hang out in the hut or go and fetch water, and at night they'd hunt endermen. There wasn't much to do during the days, so they'd tell each other stories about their adventures.

"I can't believe you've met the legendary Steve," Biff said, as Dave was recounting how Steve had helped them defeat Robo Steve in the snow. "He was always my hero growing up."

On the morning of the sixth day, Dave awoke to find Biff and the other Ender Hunters packing up their stuff and dismantling the hut.

"That's enough ender pearls for now," he said. "We'll be able to make a pretty penny down at Diamond City. You should come with us, become a real Ender Hunter. You'll live longer than you will hunting dragons."

"Thanks," said Dave, smiling, "but we'll stick to our quest."

"Suit yourselves, partner," said Biff. "Maybe we'll see you on the road again. Oh, and you can keep them there horses."

The Ender Hunters said their goodbyes and rode off, leaving Dave, Porkins and Carl with the two remaining horses.

"Well, there they go," said Carl. "Biff, Diff, Jiff and Niff. Or whatever their names were."

"They were nice chaps," said Porkins. "How many of those pearls do we have now?"

Dave did a quick count.

"Forty five," he said. "That should be more than enough."

"They're beautiful little things, aren't they?" said Porkins, studying one in his hand."

"Hey Porkins," said Carl, "you reckon you could hit that cactus over there? You're a good shot with an arrow, but how about pearl throwing?"

"Watch and see," grinned Porkins. "Your old pal Porkins is a terrific short—even if I do say so myself!"

He threw the pearl and, true to his word, it hit the cactus. Porkins grinned, but then suddenly he was gone—disappearing into thin air.

"Where is he?!" said Dave.

Then he heard a familiar voice nearby: "Owwww!"

Somehow Porkins was on top of the cactus. He jumped off, clutching his behind. Carl was laughing hysterically.

"What happened?" said Dave, feeling very confused.

"Throwing the pearls makes you teleport," said Carl, wiping away a tear of laughter. "I found out the other day when I accidentally dropped one."

"You little blighter," said Porkins, coming back over. He was pulling cactus needles out of his back.

"That was funny," grinned Carl, "you've got to admit."

"Hmph," said Porkins.

"Right you two," said Dave, "let's see where we have to go next."

He took out a blaze rod and an ender pearl from his bag, fusing them into an eye of ender, then he threw the eye into the air. It hovered for a moment, then zoomed off towards the horizon.

"That way," said Dave.

So they all got on their horses and rode off.

CHAPTER TWENTY

The Witch

It didn't take them long to leave the desert biome, and they soon found themselves traveling through a swamp. They rode across the discolored grass, along banks of large, shallow lakes and underneath hanging vines. Occasionally they'd come across strange blue flowers, which Dave picked, just in case they were useful for crafting.

As night began to fall, Dave was about to build a house when he saw some lights up ahead.

"It looks like a village or something over there," he said to Porkins and Carl.

"Or something that wants to eat us," said Carl.

Against Carl's wishes, they went and had a closer look. The lights were coming from a small hut, standing on wooden legs in the middle of some shallow water. Dave could just make out a villager, picking mushrooms on the shore nearby.

"Hello there!" he called. The villager turned round.

She was wearing a pointy hat and robes.

A witch! Dave thought. The only other witch he'd ever seen had been his grandmother, and that had been a long time ago, when he was very small.

"Hello dearie," the witch said with a smile. "It's nice to see a friendly face, I don't get many visitors all the way out here."

Carl and Porkins walked over to Dave.

"Watch out!" the witch yelled. "It's a creeper!"

"Oh, that's just Carl," laughed Dave. "Don't worry, he's friendly."

"Relatively speaking," said Carl.

The witch invited them all into her hut, and she set about cooking them some dinner in a cauldron.

"Is creeper stew ok?" she asked.

Carl's face went white. The witch giggled. "Just a little joke," she said, "it's actually pumpkin."

"Will it protect us from endermen?" laughed Porkins.

"I don't get it," said the witch.

She dished up the stew and put it down in front of them.

"Yum!" said Porkins, shoving spoonfuls of stew into his mouth as fast as he could.

"So, who are you boys then?" the witch asked, sitting down on the table next to them. "What brings you to my swamp?"

"I'm Porkins," said Porkins, "And this is Carl and Dave."

Dave could have sworn that when Porkins said *Dave* the witch's eyes went wide. It had only been for a second, but she'd definitely reacted to his name.

I must be imagining things, he thought. *I've been on the road too long, I'm starting to see things!*

"And we're on a mission to kill the ender dragon," continued Porkins.

"Really," said the witch, "how interesting. Oh my manners, I haven't introduced myself yet—I'm Dotty."

"Nice to meet you Dotty," said Dave. "Thanks so much for feeding us."

"No problem," smiled the witch. "I am curious though —how are you planning on getting to the ender dragon? I thought all the old portals were destroyed?"

"Well," said Porkins, "we have a... Dave knows a..."

Something was happening to Porkins's voice. Dave looked over and saw the pigman's eyes were starting to droop.

"Are you ok, Porkins?" Dave asked, but suddenly he began to feel incredibly tired. "I... I think I need to sleep..." he said. He looked over and saw Porkins and Carl were both already fast asleep. Porkins had fallen face first in his soup bowl. Only Dotty was still awake, and she was grinning.

"That's right, Dave, go to sleep," she said. "Go to sleep…"

And he did.

CHAPTER TWENTY-ONE

Bedrock

Dave woke up in a room with black walls. No, not quite solid black—black with flecks of gray.

Bedrock, he knew. But how could a room be made of bedrock? As far as he knew, the only place you could find bedrock was if you dug as far down as you could get. You couldn't mine it and make rooms out of it.

He was in a small cage made of iron bars, and when he looked across the room he saw Porkins and Carl in similar cages. Both of them seemed to be just waking up now too.

"What's going on now?" said Carl. "How do we always end up in these situations?"

"Gosh my head hurts," said Porkins.

Dave reached round to grab a pickaxe from his backpack—but his backpack was gone.

"Does anyone have a pickaxe?" he yelled to his friends.

Porkins reached round, then realized his backpack was gone too.

"My stuff!" the pigman said. "Some blighter has nicked it!"

"I think the same 'blighter' has taken all our stuff," said Carl.

"Your items have been confiscated," said a voice. "But if you cooperate, you may have them back."

Dave could have sworn they were alone in the bedrock room, but now there was a man in here with them, and behind him were a group of witches. One of the witches, Dave was dismayed to see, had his bag, and was flicking through the ancient book he'd found in the stronghold, back when he'd begun his adventure.

"There's nothing in here," the witch said, sounding annoyed. "Nothing about how to get to the End."

Then he noticed Dotty, the witch whose hut they'd eaten at, leaning against a wall and grinning at them.

"You!" said Dave.

"Yes, me," she grinned. "My master has been looking for you, Dave. And lucky me, you just wandered right into my home. I was just planning to rob you and your friends, to put you to sleep and steal your stuff, but when you told me your name and I realized who you were... well, I knew my master would reward me handsomely for bringing you to him."

She turned to look at the man. For a split second Dave thought the man was Steve. His voice hadn't sounded anything like Steve, but he looked the same. Apart from his eyes—this man had pure white eyes.

"Herobrine!" Porkins gasped, saying what Dave had been thinking. "You rotter! You cad! Let me out of this cage and I'll teach you—"

Herobrine waved his hand and suddenly Porkins stopped talking. But no, that wasn't quite right, Dave realized. Porkins was still talking, but no sound was coming out. It was like his voice had been stopped by magic.

Herobrine walked forward to Dave's cage. As he got closer, Dave felt an immense sense of dread and misery. It was like Herobrine's very presence was sucking all the joy from the room.

"You and your friends are all in identical cages," Herobrine said calmly. Something about his voice made the hairs on the back of Dave's neck stand on end. "Each cage has a trapdoor below it. Below the trapdoor is a lake of lava."

Dave looked down and realized, to his horror, that Herobrine was telling the truth. His cage was only one block wide and he was standing on a trapdoor, and could see the orange glow of lava through the window. There was nowhere to escape to.

"I'm going to ask you a question," Herobrine said, "and if you refuse to answer, or lie to me, the trapdoor below your creeper friend will open, and he'll fall into the lava."

"Hey, that's not fair!" said Carl. "Why can't you drop Porkins into the lava instead?"

Herobrine waved a hand, and suddenly Carl's voice was silenced, the same way Porkins's had been.

"Then I will ask you the same question again," said Herobrine. "And if you fail to answer or lie to me a second time, the pigman will go into the lava. And please don't be under any illusions—I *will* know if you're lying."

Every word that Herobrine spoke made Dave's head hurt. His voice sounded normal, but there was something horrible about it that Dave couldn't quite put his finger on. It was as if Herobrine was only pretending to look like a man and speak like a man, and that underneath was something *inhuman*—something *monstrous*.

"Finally," said Herobrine, "I will ask you the question a third time. If again you fail to give me the answer I want, *you* will go in the lava. Is that understood?"

Dave looked over at Porkins and Carl, who were both terrified.

"Listen," said Dave, "I'll tell you anything you want— please just let my friends go!"

"If you answer me true, all three of you will be released," Herobrine said softly. "You have my word."

Don't trust him! a voice in Dave's head said. And for

once it wasn't his own.

Who are you? Dave asked the voice.

It's me, Dave, the voice replied. *I'm sorry it's been so long.*

Grandma? Dave thought. He recognized the voice now—it was his grandmother. Dave hadn't seen her since he was little, but he still knew her voice.

"Is something the matter?" asked Herobrine, sounding like he was getting impatient. "I hope you appreciate the gravity of this situation."

Dave was very confused now. Not only was he captured by the mysterious Herobrine, but now he could hear his grandmother talking to him inside his head.

How are you speaking to me? Dave asked his grandmother. *Is it by magic?*

Dave didn't know much about his grandmother, but he knew she was a witch. When he was little she had always made him laugh by doing magic tricks.

Listen Dave, his grandmother's voice said, *I can't keep this up much longer, speaking to you like this is extremely difficult. Please, whatever you do, don't tell Herobrine what he wants to know. When the trapdoors open, you and your friends will be fine—I promise you. You have to trust me...*

And then her voice was gone.

"Now I will ask you my question," Herobrine said to

Dave. "Remember, if you don't answer truly, the creeper dies."

He stepped forward, staring at Dave with those horrible blank eyes.

"How do I find strongholds?" Herobrine asked.

Dave was taken aback. Was that all the question was? He was about to tell Herobrine the answer—that you had to use eyes of ender—but then he remembered what his grandmother had said.

Whatever you do, don't tell Herobrine what he wants to know.

Was he crazy to trust their lives to a strange voice inside his head? Maybe he was, but his grandmother—if it really was her—had sounded so sincere. And the other thing was, he really didn't trust Herobrine. Porkins had told Dave and Carl about how Herobrine had betrayed the pigmen, turning them all into zombies. He didn't seem like the kind of man to keep his word.

"I need an answer, please," Herobrine said.

Dave looked over at Carl. The creeper was yelling something—probably calling Dave an idiot for not just telling Herobrine what he needed to know— his voice was still silenced by Herobrine's magic.

"I'm afraid I can't help," Dave told Herobrine. "I don't know what you're talking about."

"LIAR!" spat Herobrine. His anger came so suddenly

that Dave jumped back in terror, but then he became calm again. "Pull the first lever," he said softly.

Dave noticed for the first time that there were three levers on the side of the wall. A witch grabbed one and pulled it.

There was a *click* as the trapdoor below Carl opened. The tiny creeper's mouth opened in shock, and then he was gone.

Dave saw Porkins yelling angrily at him and banging on the bars of his cell. He couldn't hear what the pigman was saying, thanks to Herobrine's magic, but he knew it was nothing nice.

I hope I'm right about this, Dave thought miserably. If he wasn't, and the voice of his grandmother had all been his imagination, then he'd just sent one of his best friends to a very nasty death.

"Now I will ask a second time," Herobrine said. "How do I find strongholds?"

"Look," said Dave, "I hate to disappoint you, but I don't know."

The look Porkins gave him almost broke his heart.

Trust me, Dave tried to tell the pigman with his eyes. *I know what I'm doing, this will all be ok.*

"Second lever!" snapped Herobrine. He'd given up the pretense of acting calm now, and Dave could see the fury all over his face.

The witch pulled the second lever and Porkins fell through. *How could you?* the look on his face seemed to be saying.

Herobrine stepped forward again, looking furious. He was so close that Dave could smell his breath. It smelled of death.

"Last chance," Herobrine hissed. "I know you've discovered a way of finding strongholds. Tell me what it is and I'll let you live. Refuse me again and you go in the lava. Got it?"

"Makes seems to me," said Dave. He was shaking he was so nervous, but he tried not to let Herobrine see.

"For the third and final time," said Herobrine, "how do I find strongholds?"

"Sorry," said Dave, "I'm afraid I can't—"

"PULL THE LEVER!" screamed Herobrine.

"Master," said Dotty anxiously, running over to him, "we can't just kill him, we need to find out what he knows!"

But Herobrine was too furious to listen.

"He refused me," he hissed, "his voice sounding less and less human by the second. "No-one refuses me! NO-ONE! Pull the lever!"

Suddenly Dave found himself falling, through the trapdoor and towards a huge lake of lava far below.

"Oh dear," he said. "I think I've made a terrible

mistake..."

CHAPTER TWENTY-TWO

Lava

Dave was falling towards the lava and there was nothing he could do about it.

Well, at least it'll be quick, he thought miserably. If the fall didn't finish him off, the lava would kill him in a few seconds.

But then he felt something grab him under the arms, and suddenly he wasn't falling anymore. He turned round and saw his savior was a witch—a witch flying with wings!

"Your grandmother sent me," the witch whispered.

"You're flying?!" Dave said stupidly.

"Keep your voice down," the witch said. "We don't want Herobrine to know you're still alive. And we're not flying, we're gliding."

Dave looked down and was surprised to see Carl and Porkins standing at the far side of the lava lake, waving at him. There were two witches with them, who, Dave realized, must have caught his friends when they fell through their trapdoors.

"So you're the good witches?" Dave said.

"We're the witches who refused to follow Herobrine," the witch said. "For years he's tried to recruit all the witches to join him, and he's done a good job. Your grandmother leads the resistance—witches who oppose Herobrine and all he stands for. I'm Miranda, by the way."

"Dave," said Dave.

Suddenly there was a blood-curdling scream of anger from behind them. Dave looked round to see a figure swoop down through one of the trapdoor holes.

"It's Herobrine!" Dave said. "And he's got wings too!"

Herobrine was flying after them, going much faster than they were.

"He's using a firework rocket for extra speed!" said Miranda.

They were near the edge of the lava lake now, where Porkins, Carl and the two witches were waiting for them. Dave noticed that there were other witches there as well, maybe ten or eleven. All of these "good" witches were wearing purple robes, unlike Herobrine's witches—who'd been wearing robes that were the same blue as his shirt.

Miranda swooped down and landed next to Porkins and Carl.

"Am I glad to see you guys!" Dave said to them. "Sorry about letting you fall into the lava—but I knew you'd be ok.

You see I heard my grandmother's voice inside my head, and she told me we'd all be safe."

Porkins and Carl gave him a funny look. Carl started to speak but stopped when he realized that no words were coming out—the silencing spell was still working, it seemed.

"TRAITORS!" Herobrine yelled, as he swooped down towards them on his rocket-powered wings. The witches all pulled out bottles of potion and started chucking them at Herobrine, but they all just splashed off him, none of them seemingly doing any damage.

"Hit his elytra!" Miranda yelled.

The witches did as she commanded, throwing their potions at Herobrine's wings. Herobrine's wings began to break, and he began spiraling down towards the lava.

"You'll all pay!" he screamed as he fell. "I'll destroy you all!"

And then *plop!* He fell into the lava and was gone.

"That was easier than I thought it would be," said Dave.

"Come on," said Miranda, "I don't think that'll hold him for long."

"Hold him?" said Dave. "He fell into lava. He's dead!"

Suddenly there was a gurgling, slurping sound behind him. Dave turned and saw something rising up from the lava. Something big.

"Run!" Miranda yelled. "Everybody into the caves!"

Dave couldn't take his eyes off the huge thing rising up from the lava. *No,* he realized with a jolt of shock. *It's not rising up from the lava—it *is* the lava!*

With slurping and slopping and a thunderous roar that echoed around the cavern, the lava monster stood up, its body starting to take shape: two arms, two legs, a body and a head with two blank eyes.

It was a giant lava Herobrine.

CHAPTER TWENTY-THREE

Giant Lava Herobrine

The huge lava Herobrine waded through the lava lake towards them. It was so tall that it had to stoop to not bump its head on the roof of the cavern.

"YOU THINK YOU CAN ESCAPE ME?!" it roared.

"Move!" Miranda said, grabbing Dave by the shoulders. He turned and saw Carl, Porkins and the witches running towards a hole in the wall of the cavern. Dave and Miranda followed them, finding themselves in a network of caves.

"Keep moving everyone!" Miranda shouted.

Suddenly the cave walls shook, as the giant lava Herobrine pounded at the wall of the cavern with his fists.

"Don't worry," said Dave, to no-one in particular. "He's too big to fit in here!"

But then his heart fell as he saw lava pouring through the cave entrance towards them.

"Keep going!" yelled Miranda. They all started running, the lava quickly catching up with them.

"Up here!" a witch said. They followed her through a narrow passageway that led upwards. They went around some twists and turns and finally found themselves in a small cave with daylight coming in from a hole in the ceiling.

"I think we lost Herobrine," said one of the witches.

"That may be, but you've found us!" said a familiar voice from above.

Dave looked up and saw Dotty and the other bad witches swooping down through the hole in the ceiling wearing elytra wings.

A huge battle broke out, the blue-robed bad witches against the good purple-robed ones. All of them throwing potions at each other or shooting each other with arrows.

"Come on!" Miranda said, grabbing Dave. "You need to get out of here!"

She led Dave, Carl and Porkins down some narrow passageways, until the sound of battle could only be heard faintly in the distance.

"You need to escape through the Nether," she told them. "Herobrine will have all the cave entrances guarded."

"I don't have obsidian," Dave told her. "Those other

witches took all our backpacks."

"Take this," Miranda said, reaching into her pockets and pulling out some tiny obsidian blocks and a piece of flint and steel. "That should be enough to get into the Nether and then get out again." She thrust it all into Dave's hands. "Now go!"

"What about you?" said Dave.

"GO!" she yelled. "If Herobrine catches you, he'll force you to reveal how to get to the End. And then we'll all be doomed." She gave his shoulder a reassuring squeeze, then ran back down the passageway, towards the battle.

Dave looked at Porkins and Carl.

"I guess we'd better go then," he said. They both nodded—both of them still unable to speak.

Dave built a rectangle of obsidian, then lit it. The liquid purple portal appeared, as it always did.

"Let's go," he said sadly. He hated the idea of leaving Miranda and the other witches behind after they'd saved their lives, but Miranda had been very insistent. For some reason she, and the other good witches, were willing to lay down their lives to stop Herobrine finding a stronghold and making his way to the End.

Dave stepped into the purple doorway. The liquid of the portal shimmered around him for a second, and then he was back in the Nether, Porkins and Carl following right behind him.

KABOOM!!

Dave was thrust forward by a huge explosion. He fell forward, landing painfully on the netherrack ground. He looked round and saw a crater where the portal had been. Carl and Porkins were on the floor next to him.

"Ow, my head," said Porkins. "Oh, I can speak again!"

"What a pity," said Carl.

"What destroyed the portal?" said Dave, getting to his feet and looking around.

And then he saw the witches. Ten or so of Herobrine's bad witches blocking the path in front of them, sitting on a huge machine made of iron blocks.

"Master Herobrine was right," a witch said gleefully. Dave recognized her as the witch who'd been looking through his backpack—and she still had it, wearing it on her back. "He thought they might try and escape through the Nether!"

"Herobrine is always right," said a tall witch, grinning nastily. "Now boys," she called down to Dave and his friends, "we have a TNT cannon aimed right at you. Come with us and no-one has to get hurt."

CHAPTER TWENTY-FOUR
Return to the Nether (Again!)

Dave needed a plan. He looked at Porkins and Carl, but they seemed as clueless as he was. What were they going to do?

"Come up here, boys," the tall witch said, sounding bored. "We've got another portal, all ready to take you back to Master Herobrine. He's *so* looking forward to seeing you again."

"Is he? That's good," said Dave, trying to play for time until he could think of a plan. Then he spotted a couple of pigmen wandering about near the remains of the portal.

"Actually," Dave told the tall witch. "We don't really fancy seeing Herobrine again. So we're just gonna go."

And he started walking towards the portal.

"What are you doing?!" Carl whispered.

"Trust me," Dave whispered back.

Reluctantly, Carl followed him. Then Porkins too.

"Stop!" the tall witch shouted at them. They heard the

squealing of metal as the TNT cannon swirled round to follow them. "We have the cannon aimed directly at you. If you don't come with us, we'll blow you to bits!"

"Nah," said Dave, "I think we're just gonna go."

"I hope you know what you're doing, old chap," said Porkins.

"You know me," said Dave, giving him a smile, "I've always got a plan."

"I'm not sure that's strictly true," said Porkins.

"Ok! You were warned!" yelled the tall witch. "FIRE!" KABOOM!!!

A blast from the TNT cannon exploded just in front of them.

"I think you missed," Dave shouted up at them.

"This is your last warming!" said the tall witch. "FIRE!!!"

This time the explosion hit the remains of the portal, blowing it to bits and the blast hitting the two zombie pigmen.

"SQUEEE!!!" they yelled as they went flying into the lava.

Suddenly there was a chorus of squealing. Dave suddenly realized there were a lot more pigmen around than he originally thought, all of them now looking agitated, making angry squealing noises and trying to look where the blast had come from.

"FIRE!" yelled the tall witch again.

"Um, are you sure?" said the witch wearing Dave's backpack. "Those pig things don't look happy..."

"I said FIRE!" the tall witch repeated.

The cannon fired again. As Dave had suspected—or at least hoped—the witches wouldn't actually fire at him, Porkins and Carl, as they wanted to bring them back to Herobrine. So the shot whizzed over Dave's head and smashed into the ground nearby, hitting some more pigmen.

This time there was no mistaking where the shot had come from. With a chorus of furious squealing, the pigmen ran angrily towards the witches.

"Uh oh," said the tall witch.

Suddenly there were dozens of angry pigmen attacking the witches from all sides. The witches started throwing potions and a huge battle broke out.

"Now, let's get out of here," Dave said to Porkins and Carl.

The three of them ran as fast as they could, weaving their way through the witches and zombie pigmen. They were coming round a corner when they heard someone shout at them from above:

"Stop right there!"

They looked up. The witch with Dave's backpack, her

clothes torn in places from the fight, was on a slope looking down at them, a potion in one hand, ready to be thrown.

"This potion will finish you in one hit," she said angrily. "I promise you that!"

But then a look of shock appeared on her face. She looked down and saw the tip of a golden sword poking through her belly.

"Oh!" she said. She fell to her knees, and then *poof!* she was gone. The pigman who'd stabbed her ran off the other way to rejoin the fight, and Dave's rucksack fell down the slope, landing by his his feet.

He grabbed it, quickly opening it to check the contents. Everything seemed to still be there—all his blocks and, more importantly, his two books. The crafting book that Old Man Johnson had given him, and the ancient book he'd found in the stronghold under his village, all that time ago—the book that had told him how to make ender eyes and find ender portals.

Dave wondered why the witch hadn't found the page about ender eyes when she'd been looking through his backpack. He opened the book and quickly scrolled to the ender eye page.

The page was blank.

Dave scrolled back and forth. He was definitely looking at the right page, but somehow all the writing and images were gone. The pages on either side were packed full of text, but the ender eye page was completely blank.

Then, right before his eyes, the text and images returned, reappearing on the page as if by magic.

It is magic, Dave thought. *The book didn't want Herobrine to know how to find the End.*

It seemed stupid, but compared to some of the crazy things Dave had seen on his adventure, a magic book was fairly low on the crazy scale.

"Are you gonna look at that book all day, or are we gonna get a move on?" said Carl.

They kept moving, walking along at a fast pace. They kept going and going until their feet hurt. There was no way of knowing how much time had passed in the Nether, so Dave didn't know if they'd been going an hour or a day.

"We must have gone far enough now," said Carl.

"I agree, dear chap," said Porkins.

So Dave built an obsidian portal, lighting it with flint and steel.

"Let's hope it brings us somewhere nice," he said, remembering the endless snow biome they'd ended up in last time.

He stepped into the portal.

CHAPTER TWENTY-FIVE

Nothing but Water

When he appeared on the other side, Dave saw clear blue skies, with barely a cloud in sight. He looked down and saw endless ocean in every direction. He was standing on a small obsidian ledge by the side of the portal—the portal had spawned in the sky, far above the water.

Aw well, he thought, *we'll just go back into the Nether and build a portal somewhere else.*

He turned to walk back into the purple liquid, when suddenly a small green thing ran through and bashed into him.

"Oops, sorry," said Carl.

Dave staggered backwards, his feet on the edge of the ledge, using his arms to try and keep balance.

"Arrrrgh!!!" said Dave.

"Uh, just hold on," said Carl. "Poker will be here in a second—he's got longer arms than me. Well, he's actually *got* arms."

Then Porkins ran through the portal.

"So where are we chaps?" he said, running straight into Carl, then straight into Dave.

"Arrrghh!!!" said Carl.

"Arrrghh!!!" said Dave.

"Oh my!" said Porkins.

And the three of them fell down, down, down, towards the water below.

EPILOGUE

Herobrine was very unhappy.

"What do you mean, they escaped?" he asked the tall witch stood in front of him.

"We went to the Nether to set a trap for them, as you asked," the witch said, her voice trembling. "But they... we were attacked by pigmen."

"Zombie pigmen, you mean?" said Herobrine. "Are you telling me you were outsmarted by zombies?"

"Not outsmarted, outnumbered."

Herobrine strode over and looked down one of the three trapdoors in the bedrock room, at the lava lake below. He'd finally had Dave the villager in his grasp, and he'd let him escape. As furious as he was with the witches, Herobrine was more furious with himself.

He'd become suspicious when Dave had so easily let his friends fall to his death. Herobrine hadn't meant to kill Dave, but he'd lost his temper. Herobrine wasn't used to being defied, and it had made him angry.

Very angry.

When Dave had fallen through the trapdoor, Herobrine had become more suspicious still. It was one thing to let your companions fall into lava, but quite another to sacrifice your own life. Herobrine had stuck his head through the trapdoor to check that Dave really had fallen to his doom, and instead saw the villager flying away, with the help of a traitorous witch.

He'd followed Dave himself, but not before sending his witches to the nearby caves and to the Nether, to cut off any escape routes. But it had all been in vain—as stupid as he looked, this *Dave* had managed to escape from Herobrine's clutches.

"Increase the search," said Herobrine. "I want every witch we have on the lookout. Search the Nether too. And take this."

He held out a golden staff with a emerald on the top.

"Master?" said the witch, sounding confused.

"This staff will let you control zombie pigmen," Herobrine told her. "What is your name, witch?"

"Isabella," said the tall witch.

"Congratulations Isabella," said Herobrine, "you're now in charge of my pigman army. I want you to summon the zombie pigmen and bring them here. They're no use to me in the Nether."

"How many shall I bring?" the witch asked, taking the staff.

"All of them," said Herobrine. "I've been operating in the shadows for too long. It's time to begin my conquest."

"What are you going to conquer?" Isabella asked.

Herobrine smiled.

"The world."

TO BE CONTINUED...

Made in the USA
Coppell, TX
04 March 2021